International Praise for Miss Read

"Miss Read reminds us of what is really important. And if we can't live in her world, it's certainly a comforting place to visit." —*USA Today*

"If you don't know Fairacre, you are twenty novels behind."
—*New York Times*

"[Miss Read] has achieved a sort of universality."
—*Chicago Sunday Tribune*

"Miss Read has three great gifts — an unerring intuition about human frailty, a healthy irony, and surprisingly, an almost beery sense of humor. As a result, her villages, the rush of the sun and snow through venerable elms, and the children themselves all miraculously manage to blend into a charming and lasting whole." —*The New Yorker*

"Humor guides her pen but it never rules it . . . Delightful."
—*Times Literary Supplement*

"We need more books like these homey stories about down-to-earth people." —*Anniston Star*

"Miss Read has created a universe in which people are kind and conscientious and courteous and manners now considered antiquated elsewhere . . . a visit to Fairacre offers a restful change from the frenetic pace of our contemporary world."
—*Publishers Weekly*

"Testimony to the gallantry of ordinary folk . . . I like Fairacre."
—*Omaha World-Herald*

"Miss Read has created a world of innocent integrity in almost perfect prose consisting of wit, humor and wisdom in equal measure."
—*Cleveland Plain Dealer*

"Someone has said she writes for ordinary people extraordinarily; when I read her I keep thinking of the acute perception and wit of Jane Austen. [Miss Read] is unique, and oh, so pleasant to read."
—*Chattanooga Times*

"Miss Read [possesses] a tranquil eye in the midst of our loud and windy times." —*Patriot Ledger*

Books by Miss Read

MRS. PRINGLE
OF FAIRACRE

Miss Read

Illustrated by J. S. Goodall

HOUGHTON MIFFLIN COMPANY
Boston   New York

First Houghton Mifflin paperback edition 2001

For information about permission to reproduce selections from
this book, write to Permissions, Houghton Mifflin Company,
215 Park Avenue South, New York, New York 10003.

Visit our Web site: www.houghtonmifflinbooks.com.

Library of Congress Cataloging-in-Publication Data
Read, Miss.
Mrs. Pringle of Fairacre
ISBN 0-618-15588-0 (pbk)
I. Title.
PR 6069.A42M58   1990B
823'.914—dc20   90-4669

Printed in the United States of America

QUM 10 9 8 7 6 5 4 3 2 1

To Vicki and Horace
with love

CHAPTER 1

Face to Face

It is snowing again. We shall certainly have a white Christmas this year, a rare occurrence even in this downland village of Fairacre.

I have been the head teacher of Fairacre School for more years than I care to remember, and the school house, where I write this, has been my home for all that time. It is particularly snug at the moment: the fire blazes, the cat is stretched out in front of it, and Christmas cards line the mantelpiece. Very soon the school breaks up for the Christmas holidays, and what a comforting thought that is!

Comfort is needed, not only from the snowflakes which whisper at the window, but also from the aftermath of a recent skirmish with Mrs Pringle, our school cleaner, who has lived in the village even longer than I have.

She does her job superbly, but is a sore trial. It is generally agreed that she is 'difficult', the vicar's expression, and 'a proper Tartar', as Bob Willet our handyman and school caretaker puts it.

During term time our paths cross on most days. It is no wonder that I relish the school holidays and the peace that they bring. How long, I muse, putting another log on the

1

fire, will I be able to stand her aggression? Stroking Tibby's warm stomach, I look back through the years at my tempestuous relationship at Fairacre School with the doughty Mrs Pringle.

I first encountered Mrs Pringle one thundery July afternoon.

It was a Friday, I remember. The vicar, the Reverend Gerald Partridge who was chairman of the school governors, had invited me to tea before looking over the school house which was to become my home at the end of the month. I had recently been appointed head mistress of Fairacre School.

There were puddles in the playground, and we splashed through them on our way to the school house. A strange mooing noise, as of a cow or calf in distress, was coming from the deserted school building. The children of Fairacre had already started their summer holiday.

'That,' said Mr Partridge, 'is Mrs Pringle, our school cleaner. It sounds as though she is singing a hymn. She is in the church choir.'

We paused for a moment, listening to the distant voice and the plop of raindrops into puddles.

'I don't recognise it,' I ventured.

'Probably the descant,' replied the vicar. He did not sound very sure. 'In any case, perhaps I should take you to meet her before we visit the house.'

We changed direction, and the vicar pushed open the door into the lobby.

Mrs Pringle, bucket at her feet and floor cloth in the other, stood before us. She was short and stout. Her expression was dour. She made no attempt to smile, offer a hand, or make any other gesture of welcome as the vicar introduced us.

Eventually, she jerked her head towards the floor where our feet had made wet prints.

'I just done that,' she remarked, the four words dropping as cold and flat as the stones upon which we stood.

Although I did not know it at the time, it was the first shot in a war which was to last for many years.

I was the first woman to be appointed head teacher of Fairacre School, and I looked forward eagerly to taking up my duties.

The downland village and the market town of Caxley were known to me, for my good friend Amy who had been with me at college, had married and lived south of Caxley in the village of Bent. On my frequent weekend visits we explored the countryside, and often drove up to the downs for a picnic and an exhilarating walk. We drove through the villages of Beech Green and Fairacre and sometimes stopped to look round their churches, or to buy something from Beech Green's village shop.

When I had seen the headship of Fairacre School advertised in *The Times Educational Supplement* I had applied for the post.

'I'm not likely to get it,' I said to Amy, 'I doubt if I shall even get called to an interview.'

'Rubbish!' said Amy stoutly. 'You are better qualified than most, and I'm positive you'll get the job.'

Although I was grateful for this display of support, biased though it was, I had private misgivings. Consequently, when I was appointed, I felt both pride and trepidation. Could I fulfil the governors' hopes, and would the children and parents be co-operative?

I need not have worried.

Any initial suspicions or doubts on the part of the

inhabitants of Fairacre were soon hidden from me, and as the years passed I was accepted as part of the village community. I could never expect to be in the same category as a native, born and bred in Fairacre, but to be welcomed was quite enough for me.

But on that humid thundery afternoon I was still at the apprehensive stage, and my encounter with the school cleaner aroused my fears.

I tried to put them aside as I followed the vicar round my new home. It was a snug well-built house with a good-sized sitting room, and a decent kitchen flanked by a small dining room. Upstairs were two bedrooms and a tiny box room, later destined to be a bathroom.

At that time the house was empty, for my predecessor, Mr Fortescue, had moved out just before his retirement. It was Mrs Pringle, the vicar told me, who had a key and kept the premises clean.

'In fact,' went on the vicar, 'she has cared for this house for many years.'

'I see,' I said, my heart sinking.

'Of course, it is entirely up to you, but if you felt like continuing to employ her, I am sure she would carry on.'

'Thank you for telling me.'

'She is really a wonderful worker,' persisted the vicar as we went out into the dripping garden. 'Her manner is a little off-putting, I know, but she is diligent and honest, and has always taken a great pride in her work.'

I did not reply, determined not to commit myself at this stage, to being hostess to Mrs Pringle for years to come.

'What a lovely garden!' I said, changing the subject.

There were a few mature fruit trees displaying small unripe apples, plums and pears, and an impressive herbaceous border flaunting lupins, delphiniums and oriental poppies.

The flowers were looking rather battered from the recent rain, the border was undoubtedly weedy and the lawn shaggy, but basically it was a splendid garden, and my spirits rose.

'Yes, Mr Willet gives a hand,' said the vicar. 'In fact, he gives a hand at most of our activities, as you will find.'

He drew out a watch from his waistcoat pocket.

'Dear, dear! I think we should get back to the vicarage. My wife will have tea ready.'

We retraced our steps to rejoin Mrs Partridge and Amy who had brought me over, and who had spent the time, I learned later, in unravelling the sleeve of a cardigan which the vicar's wife was engaged upon. She had misread the directions for increasing, and the sleeve was ballooning out

5

in an alarming fashion, to say nothing of using up all the wool before the whole thing was finished.

As the vicar and I walked up the drive to our tea he returned to the subject of Mrs Pringle.

'Do consider the matter of employing her,' he urged. 'I feel sure she is expecting it.'

He sounded, I thought, somewhat nervous. Was he *frightened* of the lady, I wondered? Was she really as fearsome as she undoubtedly looked? It only strengthened my determination not to commit myself.

'I'll certainly consider it,' I assured him, as he opened the front door.

'Ah, good!' he replied, sounding much relieved. 'And good again, I think I can smell toasted teacakes.'

On the way back to Bent, I prattled happily to Amy about the school house and garden, and how much I looked forward to living there.

'You must let me give you a hand in getting it ready,' said Amy, hooting at a pheasant who strolled haughtily across the road intent on suicide.

'I should enjoy your company,' I replied.

'It's not so much my *company*,' said Amy severely, 'as my *advice* you will need. You know you've never been much good at measuring accurately, and I haven't much opinion of your sense of colour.'

'Thank you,' I said, trying not to sound nettled. That is the worst of friends who have known you from youth. They remember all those faults which one has done one's best to eradicate over the years. However, Amy always means well, despite her undoubted bossiness, and on this occasion I managed not to answer back.

In any case, I reminded myself, I had quite a few

memories of Amy's early indiscretions, and should have no hesitation in using them if she continued to rake up the infirmities in my own past.

But I was too euphoric about my future to take serious offence as Amy's car swished through the puddles. The sky remained lowering, and it was obvious that the thunderstorm was not yet over.

'Of course, the garden needs tidying,' I continued, 'but the vicar seems to think that someone called Bob Willet will give a hand. I must get in touch with him.'

'And what about the house?'

I felt a slight pang as I recalled Mrs Pringle's visage, quite as dark and menacing as the sky overhead.

'Well,' I began, 'the school cleaner seems to have looked after the head teacher's house before, but I didn't really take to her.'

'Taking to her or not,' said Amy, 'is beside the point. You're not exactly the model housewife, as you well know. I should advise you to take whatever domestic help is offered.'

'But, Amy,' I protested, 'you haven't seen this Mrs Pringle. She's quite formidable. Why, I believe the vicar himself is afraid of her, and after all he's girt about with righteousness and all the other Christian armament. What hope for a defenceless woman like me?'

'You exaggerate,' replied Amy, swinging neatly into her drive. 'I'll come over with you next time and meet the lady.'

And what a clash of the dinosaurs that could be, I thought with some relish as I clambered from the car.

James, Amy's husband, proved to be a welcome ally later that evening when the subject of help in my new abode cropped up.

'I shouldn't saddle myself with that lady if I were you,' he said. 'Fob her off. Say you want to see how things work out. Play for time.'

'My feelings entirely,' I responded. 'I didn't like to press Mr Partridge too much. He seems so anxious not to offend her, but perhaps a few discreet enquiries among other villagers would be useful. This Bob Willet might be helpful.'

'There are no such things as *discreet enquiries* in a village,' said James. 'Everything is known within a flash. I should make up your own mind. Keep your ears open, by all means, but your mouth shut. I was brought up in a village and I know what I'm talking about.'

'I've had some experience of living in a village myself,' I responded, 'but not as one of the pillars of society as I suppose I will be in Fairacre. I shall have to watch my step.'

'If you are going to be a public figure,' remarked Amy, 'and an example of right living to the children and their parents, I should think that a clean house might be the first step in the right direction.'

She sounded rather waspish, I thought, probably rather cross with James for taking my part.

'Well, I haven't turned down Mrs Pringle absolutely flat,' I pointed out, 'but I'm not being rushed into anything.'

'Wise girl,' commented James.

Amy gave a snort.

In bed later, I recalled the pleasures of my first sight of the school house and garden. It gave me great joy to remember the pleasant rooms awaiting my furniture, and the pretty garden awaiting urgent attention by both Bob Willet and me.

I refused to be put off by the malevolent shade of Mrs Pringle.

'A mere fly in the ointment,' I said aloud, settling into my pillow.

I fell asleep within minutes.

CHAPTER 2

Settling In

What with one thing and another, it was the beginning of August before I could make my next visit to Fairacre.

Amy, hospitable as ever, was going to put me up, but I made the journey by train, and then caught one of the rare buses which went from Caxley to Fairacre.

It was market day in the little town, and the stall holders were doing a brisk trade in the square. It was hot and noisy, and my case was heavy. I was glad to climb aboard the bus and find a seat.

Fairacre was several miles distant, and the bus chugged gently uphill from the valley of the river Cax, stopping at the villages for laden shoppers to alight.

At Beech Green, the village before Fairacre, the bus stopped beside the village school, and I wondered who my next door colleague might be.

It was a scorching afternoon, the very best time to see this downland country. In some distant fields, harvest had already started, combines crawling like gigantic toys around the fields.

The hedges were heavy with summer foliage, still starred

here and there with late wild roses and the creamy flat heads of elderflowers. The grass on the roadside banks was sun-bleached, and as the bus swished by it undulated like ripe corn before a strong wind.

Amy was coming to pick me up at the school house at half past four, and meanwhile I had over two hours in which to visit Mr Willet, the Post Office and, best of all, my new house and garden.

It was no wonder that my spirits were high as we rattled towards Fairacre.

Mr Willet was hoeing in his remarkably neat vegetable patch. Despite the heat he was wearing a cap, and although he was in his shirt sleeves he had a tweed waistcoat as his outer garment.

After greetings and my compliments on his vegetables, I

broached the subject of help in the garden at the school house.

'Now I was hopin' you'd be along,' said Mr Willet. 'I've looked after that for more years than I can count. It may look a bit rough at the moment, as I didn't like to be too forward and trespass-like in there when I'd not been given permission.'

'But you'll come?'

'Of course I'll come. Be up tomorrow evenin' if you like. There's a row of shallots should be lifted by now. I wondered if I ought to do that, but thought Mrs Pringle might catch sight of me and tell all and sundry I was pinchin' 'em.'

This gave me an opening for further enquiries.

Mr Willet pushed back his cap and leant heavily on the hoe.

'Let's put it this way. I don't like to speak ill of anyone,' he began, obviously about to do just that, 'but you wants to start as you means to go on with that one. I'm not sayin' she's all bad. She done a lot for us when my Alice was took ill one winter, but she's a proper moaner. If you gets a smile out of her, you'll be the first as has.'

'Well, thank you for telling me. Forewarned is fore-armed, so they say.'

'It isn't *arms* as is the trouble with her. It's *legs*. She's got one that gives her a mort of trouble, so she says, and everyone else too come to that, when she's crossed in any way. Ah, yes! Mrs Pringle's leg is a force to be reckoned with, as you'll find.'

We walked together to the gate.

'You lettin' her do your house-cleanin'?' he asked, coming to the point with a directness I already respected.

'I haven't decided . . .'

'You think it over well, Miss Read. 'Tis easy enough to ask people in, and a durn sight more tricky to get 'em out. Not that she isn't a good worker, I will say that,' he added.

'I'll be over tomorrow evening,' I promised, 'and we'll look at the garden together.'

'I'll tell Alice you called. She's over at Springbourne on some W.I. lark. She'll want to hear all about you.'

And so will the rest of Fairacre, I surmised, as I made my way to the Post Office.

After the few obligatory comments on the weather (nice to see the sun, but the peas need some rain to plump up), I introduced myself to Mr Lamb.

'Hope you'll be very happy here,' he said, shaking my hand. 'Thought it was you getting off the bus. Been to see Bob Willet?'

'As a matter of fact I have.'

'Good chap, Bob. Going to give you a hand in the garden?'

'I hope so.'

'Nothing that chap can't turn his hand to. Looks after the school a fair treat, and the church and graveyard. And always cheery.'

He stopped suddenly. 'You met Mrs Pringle yet?'

I said that I had.

'She'll be cleaning the school still, I suppose?'

I said that I hoped so.

'Excuse me asking, but is she going to work for you too? In the house, I mean?'

I said that I had not yet made up my mind.

Mr Lamb gave a sigh. It sounded like one of relief.

'Yes, well. She's a good worker, I'll grant, but I'd take time in deciding to have her regular myself.'

13

I thanked him, bought some stamps and a packet of biscuits, and made my way to the school house.

Amy had already arrived, and was wandering about the garden. She was smiling in a dreamy fashion.

'What a blissful spot. Absolute peace!'

There was an ancient bench lodged against the house wall. It looked as though it had once been part of the furnishings of Fairacre School in Queen Victoria's reign. We settled ourselves upon it, turning our faces up to the sun.

Some shaggy Mrs Sinkin pinks wafted their scent towards us. Two inquisitive chaffinches surveyed us within a yard of our feet, and far away some sheep bleated from the downland.

'"To sit in the shade and look upon verdure,"' I quoted.

'Except that we're not in the shade,' Amy pointed out, 'and I shall be done to a frizzle if I stay here too long. By the way, I brought a flask of tea.'

'You marvellous girl! And I've got some Rich Tea biscuits.'

'My word, you are going it,' commented Amy.

'Well, it was either Rich Tea or Garibaldi from the Post Office, so I settled for Rich Tea. After all, they'll do for cheese as well.'

'Very prudent,' said Amy.

She went to the car to fetch the flask, and I hastily shifted my weight to the centre of the bench, which bucked alarmingly when Amy left it.

'We could have it inside,' I said. 'I've got the key.'

'Better out here,' Amy replied, 'besides, I don't suppose there's anything to sit on in there.'

She was quite right – of course.

We sipped our tea. The chaffinches had flown to a nearby plum tree, but kept a sharp lookout for crumbs.

'Of course, you'll have to put in a lot of work on this garden,' said Amy, becoming her usual brisk self, 'it's been terribly neglected.'

I told her about my visit to Mr Willet.

'Sounds hopeful,' she conceded. 'And this Mrs Pringle?'

As if on cue, I heard the click of the garden gate and round the corner of the house stumped a thickset figure with a black oilcloth bag over her arm.

Mrs Pringle had arrived.

I made the necessary introductions and awaited the outcome with some interest.

We had both risen at the approach of our visitor and I invited her to share the bench.

'I wish I could offer you tea,' I apologised, 'but I'm afraid it's all gone. Have a biscuit.'

Mrs Pringle held up a hand as if she were stopping the traffic. 'I don't eat between meals. It don't do the digestion any good.'

There seemed to be no adequate reply to this dictum.

'I was just passing,' went on the lady, 'and thought I'd put this week's *Caxley Chronicle* through your door. No doubt you'd like to be up to date with what's happening. Fairacre news is on page six.'

'Thank you. Very kind of you. I will let you have it back.'

'No need for that. I've read all I want. I always turns to the Deaths first, and then the Wills, and if anybody local's up in Caxley court I sees what they've got. Not much usually. Probation or some such let-off, when a nice bit of flogging would be more to the point.'

I put the newspaper on the small space between Amy and me, and resolutely avoided catching my old friend's eye.

'Garden looks a real mess,' she continued lugubriously. 'I happened to see you going into Bob Willet's just now, so I suppose he'll be up to give you a hand.'

'That's right.'

'So I heard at the Post Office when I called in just now.'

The bench shuddered at Amy's ill-concealed mirth.

'Would you like to look round the garden?' I asked.

'Well, I knows it like the back of my hand, of course,' replied Mrs Pringle, 'but it'd be nice to get out of this blazing sun for a few minutes, and there should be a few gooseberries about still.'

Amy accompanied us. Despite the heat, the long grass was damp, and Amy examined her elegant sandals.

'Hot or not,' observed Mrs Pringle, 'I always wears good sensible shoes. My mother brought us up to respect our feet. "Nothing strappy or silly," she used to say, "or you'll be storing up trouble for your old age." And she was right.'

At this double insult to her footwear and her advancing years Amy could only respond with some heavy breathing. So far, I thought, Mrs Pringle was winning hands down.

There certainly were some fine late gooseberries at the end of the garden, yellow translucent beauties dangling from the thorny branches.

Mrs Pringle eyed them greedily.

'Do help yourself to a picking,' I said, 'if you could use some.'

'Very nice of you,' she replied, still unsmiling. 'Lucky I brought my bag.'

Amy and I helped, but Mrs Pringle's speed at gooseberry-picking was amazing. Within ten minutes, three bushes were stripped and the oilcloth bag almost full.

She straightened up reluctantly. 'I must say I like a nice gooseberry pie,' she said, 'and now I'd best be off. Pringle gets in about now.'

At the gate she stopped.

'I take it you'll need me on a Wednesday afternoon to do your house over? Been doing it for years now. If Wednesdays don't suit, what about Tuesdays?'

I took a deep breath. 'Can I let you know? I should like to see if I can manage on my own for a bit. But thank you for the offer.'

For the first time that afternoon, she looked taken aback. 'Are you saying you don't want me?'

17

'Not at the moment. Let's see how things go.'

Without a word she opened the gate and set off down the lane, her heavy bag swinging dangerously.

'Well!' exploded Amy. 'What a miserable old faggot!'

This archaic expression from my childhood days made me laugh.

'So *rude*,' continued Amy, 'criticizing my sandals! And greedy too! Why, she's got enough gooseberries there to make *two dozen* pies.'

'So you don't take to Mrs P? She did offer to help in the house, you know.'

'I thought you handled that very well,' said Amy, with rare praise. 'Personally, I wouldn't employ her for a pension, the wicked old harridan.'

'Let's unlock the house and have a look round. It might lower our blood pressure after that encounter.'

'We certainly need something,' agreed Amy, following me.

Later that evening we discussed the afternoon's events, and made our plans for the next few days.

Amy had volunteered to help me paint the downstairs walls. Upstairs, we agreed, could wait until later. We proposed to go into Caxley in the morning and choose emulsion paint and brushes, and also to buy curtaining material for the main living room, at present my predecessor's dining room. For all Amy's elegance, she was a great one for practical pursuits and I welcomed her co-operation in the decorating project.

My furniture was due to arrive at the end of the week and, all being well, we should have the house clean and ready for it.

'Without Mrs Pringle's assistance?' queried James, much

amused by his wife's volte-face on the employment of Mrs Pringle in my house.

'Absolutely without!' snapped Amy.

'I bet she comes along to see what we're doing though,' I prophesied.

'If I know anything about village life, she won't be the only one,' rejoined James.

He was right. Over the next few days, as Amy and I toiled with our brushes and some rather exquisite pale grey paint, we had several visitors.

The first was more than welcome, for it was Bob Willet.

'I really come up to get your twitch out,' he volunteered.

It sounded rather a medical matter until Amy said she had far too much couch grass in her border, and I remembered the country name for this wretched weed.

'But I could give you a hand in here instead,' he offered, looking at the half-done walls and then the floor boards.

'You wants to wipe up with a bit of damp rag as you go,' he said. 'Shall I take a turn?'

'No, no,' we protested, 'you carry on in the garden, and we'll muddle along in here.'

He went rather reluctantly.

Our next visitor was the milkman, a cheerful young man with a splendid black beard, who said he would come on Monday, Wednesday and Saturday if that was all right?

We said it was.

'And if I was you,' he added, looking at the floor, 'I'd wipe up that paint as it falls.'

An hour later, Mrs Partridge, the vicar's wife, called in and gave us a welcome invitation to tea any time between four and five.

'Just when you've finished one wall, or something,' she said vaguely, 'in fact whenever it's convenient to stop.'

She admired our handiwork in a most satisfactory way, and only noticed the floor as she went out.

'Ah now! I believe Bob Willet carries a piece of wet cloth with him when he does work for us, and he wipes up the paint as he goes along. He says it saves a lot of trouble later.'

We said that he had been kind enough to pass on this tip already.

At two-thirty, Mrs Pringle appeared, paused on the threshold, and drew a deep breath.

'Oh dear, oh dear!' she groaned, shaking her head. 'My poor floor!'

I did not like to point out that it was in fact *my* floor, but invited her in to see our efforts. She approached gingerly, stepping over the larger blobs of paint with exaggerated care.

'I didn't come in here to pry,' she said unnecessarily, 'but as I was going over to the school to check the supplies was all right for next term, I thought I'd just look in.'

'Well, what do you think of it?' I asked, inviting the bolt from the blue.

'It'll show the dirt,' she said, and departed.

The rest of the summer holiday was spent mainly in getting the house to rights. As all those who have moved house know, nothing was straightforward.

Two of the windows were stuck fast, and needed Mr Willet and a hefty friend to release them, breaking one pane in the process. It meant a trip to Caxley for more glass.

The man who laid the stair carpet forgot to put the

underlay down first, the excuse being that his wife had given birth to twins in the early hours of the morning and it had unsettled him. I wondered what it had done to his wife.

The removal men were three hours late and made a mark on the beautiful new dove-grey paint. A nasty scratch had appeared on the side of my dressing table, but the men assured me that if I put it 'best side to London', meaning with that side against a wall, where I did not want it, then all would be well.

I never did find the tea cosy or the egg timer. My guess is that they went back in the van.

But gradually things were sorted out, and I grew fonder and fonder of my home as the days passed. Callers still dropped in with some excuse or other, and I was proud to show them over my new abode.

I also paid a few calls myself, and one of them was to see Miss Clare who lived at Beech Green, and would be my only member of staff and sole companion in our labours together. I had taken to her at first sight, when I had come for the interview some months earlier. It had been a great comfort to know that Miss Clare, who had taught at Fairacre for many years, would be there as my support when I took up the post.

Her cottage could have graced any of the 'Beautiful Britain' type of calendar. It had been thatched first by her father, and the straw renewed by a young local man who was making his name as a master thatcher.

The garden was the perfect cottage mixture of summer flowers at the front and a vegetable patch and lawn at the back. There were even hollyhocks doing their best to reach up to the eaves, with pansies and pinks at their feet.

In the distance, the downs shimmered in a blue haze of heat,

21

and I was glad to prop my bicycle against the fence, and to sit in the cool sitting room. A fat tabby cat basked on the window sill, a lark poured forth a torrent of song above the field beyond the garden, and I could understand the inner peace which gave Dolly Clare such strength and calm.

She was a tall slender woman, dressed this afternoon in a dark blue linen frock which high-lighted her white hair and pale skin.

She had been a pupil at Fairacre School, and had then gone on to become a pupil teacher, encouraged by the head master of that time Mr Wardle, who recognised in this quiet fourteen-year-old the makings of a first-class teacher. She and her life-long friend Emily Davis had

trained together, and both taught locally for many years, known officially as 'uncertificated teachers' but, like so many thus designated, were efficient, dedicated and much-loved by pupils and parents.

The vicar had told me all this. It was plain that he had a high regard for Miss Clare, as I had too.

We discussed a few practical matters concerned with the timetable and then, inevitably, the subject of Mrs Pringle cropped up. I told her that I had decided to postpone any firm invitation to the lady about working in the school house, and she nodded approval.

'She's not an easy person, as no doubt you've guessed. In any case, the position now is rather different. When we had a head master it was the wife who coped with the domestic side. Now you have to deal with her at school and in your home. Very wise to take it step by step.'

'Why is she so difficult?'

Miss Clare smiled. 'I expect present-day psychologists would blame some childhood drama, or even heredity, as no one these days seems to accept the fact that evil is as rife today as ever it was.'

'I wouldn't have labelled Mrs P. as evil,' I protested, 'just a bit of a misery.'

'That's true. But why she is such a misery is a mystery. I suppose I've known her longer than most people in Fair-acre.'

'Did you teach her?'

'No. She was brought up in Caxley. Born there too, I believe, and was the first child. But she had relations in Fairacre, an aunt and uncle, though whether they were blood relatives or simply friends of her parents, I don't know, but they used to have her for visits during the school holidays, so I used to see her about.'

'What was she like as a child?'

'Much the same as she is today,' said Dolly Clare, looking amused. 'The first time I came across her, she had been sent to this aunt because the next child was coming into the world. She was particularly resentful, but we all put it down to temporary jealousy, quite common on these occasions.'

'Did it pass?'

'No, I can't say it did. And when another baby turned up, it made things worse. Mind you, I don't think the two younger children were the reason for Maud being so gloomy. I realise now that she was that by nature, and time has proved it.'

'Well, I'm glad to know that my reaction to the lady is pretty general. And I'm glad to know her name is Maud!'

'But don't dare to call her by it,' warned Miss Clare. 'She would look upon that as terribly familiar! No, "Mrs Pringle" it must be, I assure you.'

I promised to remember.

On the night before term began, as I prepared for bed, I thought how lucky I was to have obtained this post in Fairacre. I had already made friends with Dolly Clare, Bob Willet, the kind vicar and his wife, and was on nodding terms with most of the other local inhabitants.

My house was as straight as one could reasonably expect in the time, although the new curtains, being made by someone Amy had recommended, were still not done, and there was a strange ticking noise at night which I could not track down, and only prayed that it was not something gruesome like death watch beetle at work.

The school gleamed from Mrs Pringle's labours, and a

strong smell of yellow soap, mingled with carbolic disinfectant, greeted one as the door opened.

The stocks of books, stationery, and educational apparatus seemed adequate, but I had been busy with a list of further requirements which I hoped would soon be forthcoming.

All in all, I climbed into bed that night in a hopeful frame of mind. Amy had once said: 'Will you feel lonely out there in the wilds?' I could truthfully say that I had been so enchanted with my house and garden, the village and the glorious countryside surrounding it, that I had not felt the faintest qualm of loneliness.

And tomorrow, I had no doubt that I should have other responsibilities which were equally absorbing. I was not so euphoric as to imagine that all would go smoothly. There would be frustrations and annoyances, possibly hostility from parents who preferred Mr Fortescue's régime, but these thoughts did not stop me from sleeping from ten o'clock until nearly seven the next morning.

CHAPTER 3

Bob Willet Remembers

There was no doubt about it, as all agreed, Mrs Pringle was a good worker.

Her chief passion was a fierce proprietory love of the two coke-burning stoves which dominated the infants' room and my own. These monsters had heated the school throughout many winters extremely efficiently. Each was surrounded by a sturdy fireguard which had a brass top running round it. On this we dried gloves, socks, tea towels, scarves and very useful it was.

In bitterly cold weather I warmed the children's milk in a saucepan kept for the purpose. Children with earache or toothache were placed with the afflicted area close to the stove's blessed warmth. All in all, each provided the classroom with much varied comfort.

But Mrs Pringle's attitude towards these charges of hers went far beyond our general gratitude and affection. Like the Romans, she had her household gods, and top of the list were Fairacre School's two coke stoves.

She did her duty conscientiously with the desks, cupboards, floors and so on, and also came to wash up the dinner things. Everything sparkled, tea towels were snowy,

26

the zeal with which she laboured was highly commendable. But it was the stoves which meant most to her.

At the beginning of the term they had shone like jet with lots of blacklead and Mrs Pringle's elbow grease. The cast-iron lids were much indented with a pattern, and by dint of skilful use of a blacklead brush these ornamentations stood out splendidly.

A light dusting was really all that was needed to keep them in pristine condition for the first few weeks. Even so, I noticed that the blacklead brush appeared now and again to keep them just as Mrs Pringle wanted.

We were lucky with the weather, and it was not until half term that the first chill winds of October began to blow.

I had been looking forward to tidying up the garden. Fallen leaves were strewn everywhere, and the dead spires of lupins, delphiniums and other summer plants needed cutting down. The lawns were in need of mowing and edging, and the plum tree had surpassed itself with a harvest of yellow fruit which bid fair to nourish the whole village.

But my plans were frustrated by the weather. Rain lashed across the garden, the distant downs were invisible, and it was so cold that I lit a fire in my sitting room.

Amy rang to see how I was getting on, and I vented my frustration into her listening ear.

'As Burns says: "The best laid schemes of mice and men gang aft agley",' she quoted.

I was not comforted. 'Well my schemes certainly have "ganged agley",' I told her. 'What about yours?'

'We're off to a wedding tomorrow, and apart from a mackintosh, wellingtons and a sou-wester, I can't think what to wear.'

27

'Thermal underwear for a start, and then anything warm under the mac.'

'I expect you're right. And how are things with you? Is Mrs Pringle still playing up?'

'Mrs Pringle,' I said forcefully, 'will be lighting the school stoves this week, come hell or high water, if this weather lasts.'

'Attagirl!' said Amy, putting down the receiver.

School began on the Tuesday. I saw Mrs Pringle sloshing through the puddles in the playground soon after eight that morning. She was wearing a raincoat, wellingtons and a shiny plastic head square, and carried the usual oilcloth bag on her arm.

I snatched a coat from the peg on the kitchen door and sped after her. She was busy unlocking the school when I caught up.

'Mrs Pringle! Let's get inside and out of this downpour.'

We gained the comparative peace of my classroom. A pool of water lay on the floor immediately below the skylight in the roof. It was my first encounter with a problem which would be with me throughout my teaching years at Fairacre School.

'Good heavens!' I exclaimed. 'We must get this seen to.'

Mrs Pringle gave something between a snort and a sarcastic laugh.

'That there skylight *has been seen to* more times than I can remember,' she told me, with considerable satisfaction, 'and nothing don't make no difference.'

'Do you mean it has leaked for years?'

'Every winter. Every drop of rain. Every storm. Every snow shower . . .'

'But it can't be beyond the wit of man to put it to

rights,' I broke in before Mrs Pringle called upon all the armoury of the heavens to prove her point.

'It's beyond the wit of Bob Willet,' she said, 'and if he can't fathom it, there's none else can. Why, we've even had people out from Caxley, *sent by The Office* what's more, and they've been beat.'

'Well, we shall have to try again,' I said. 'It was sheer luck that it didn't drip all over my desk.'

'Most head teachers have shifted this 'ere desk along a bit when it starts raining. Only needs a bit of forethought,' she said rudely.

I ignored the thrust, and gave one of my own.

'I came over early to say we'd better have the stoves alight now.'

'The stoves? *Alight?*' gasped the lady. 'What, in this weather?'

'Particularly in this weather.'

'But it's still October!'

'I really don't care if it is June, Mrs Pringle. The children can't work in this temperature, and I don't intend to let them try.'

'But what will The Office say?''

'What the Office says I can well answer,' I said, beginning to lose patience. 'All I am asking is that you will be good enough to put a match to each of the stoves. I know you have set them already, and Mr Willet has brought in coke.'

Mrs Pringle's face began to be suffused with an unpleasant shade of red, and her bosom heaved as busily as a Regency heroine's. I began to wonder, with some alarm, how one dealt with an apoplectic fit, and wished, not for the first time, that I had undertaken that course in first-aid which I kept postponing.

29

But her voice came out steadily and with such malevolence that Miss Clare's talk of evil rushed into my mind.

'You knows what you are starting, I suppose? It's not just *a match* as is needed, it's cleaning out, setting again, clearing up the mess, heaving in the coke, day in and day out for months to come. And all when there's *no need*.'

'But there is need,' I said as bravely as I could under this onslaught. I was ashamed to feel my legs beginning to shake, and my inside becoming decidedly queasy. There was no doubt about it, Mrs Pringle was a formidable enemy. I could see how she barged her way, like a tank, through village affairs.

'And what about my poor leg?' she thundered, thrusting her furious face close to mine.

I retreated hastily, stepping into the puddle. 'What about it?' I countered.

'Doctor Martin says I'm to respect my leg. It flares up if I overdoes it, and seeing to these stoves isn't going to help.'

I summoned all my failing strength. 'In that case, should you be doing this job? I've no wish to impose on an invalid, but these stoves must be lit this morning.'

Mrs Pringle drew in an outraged breath, ready for a renewed attack, but I made a swift exit with as much dignity as I could muster, and was thankful to return to my kitchen, and a cup of coffee which did little to calm my shattered nerves.

But the stoves were lit.

I was conscious that Mrs Pringle's leg was being dragged along heavily for the rest of the day, and an ominous silence hung over any chance meeting we had, but I refused to offer an olive branch. If she wanted to sulk then that suited me; as long as she did her work that was really

31

all that mattered. I was not going to pander to Mrs Pringle's feelings, or her leg.

Mr Willet came up that evening bearing two large marrows which would have been enough for a family of twelve, let alone one spinster. I thanked him effusively and invited him in.

'Well, just for half a minute,' he said, wiping his boots vigorously on the kitchen mat. 'I see you've managed to get the stoves goin'.'

I had suspected that this visit was not only to deliver two marrows. Now I knew his real motive.

'Well, it was cold enough,' I said. I was careful to remain unforthcoming. Village prattle grows as it spreads, like bindweed.

'But I bet you had a battle with our Mrs Sunshine,' responded Mr Willet, unabashed.

I confessed that I had.

'You don't want to worry overmuch about her feelin's,' he said, sturdily. 'She's been the same since she was so high.'

He held a horny hand six inches from the floor.

'Always a tartar, that one. Why, I can tell you how I first rumbled our Mrs Pringle, and I bet she remembers it as well as I do.'

'But I oughtn't to keep you,' I began weakly.

Bob Willet settled back in his chair. 'It was like this,' he said.

As a child, Bob Willet had lived in a cottage between the villages of Springbourne and Fairacre. There were several children, and Bob's mother was well known as a fine disciplinarian, a good mother and an exemplary housewife.

In Springbourne itself was another family, the Picketts,

32

who did not come up to Mrs Willet's high standards. One of the sons, Ted Pickett, attended Fairacre School and often called on his way to pick up the Willet children.

Mrs Willet senior was not best pleased at this attention, and hoped that Bob's obvious admiration for Ted, a year or two older than he was, would soon fade. But the friendship grew stronger as the days passed, and Bob's mother resigned herself to the inevitable.

One day, in the summer holidays when Bob was about eight and Ted nearing ten, the two boys wandered into Fairacre and sat on a sunny bank by the roadside.

In those days there was a sizeable duck pond in Fairacre, and the boys watched the ducks going about their lawful occasions. It was too hot to be energetic, and the lads were content to loll back chewing grass and wishing they had a penny, or even a halfpenny, to buy liquorice strips or four gob-stoppers from the village shop.

Before long, a little girl about Bob's age appeared on the other side of the pond where a duck board sloped from the further bank into the water. She took up her position at the top of the board and made clucking noises. The ducks, excited and trusting, rushed towards her in a flurry of wings and water.

'Wotcher!' shouted Ted, languidly.

'Who is she?' asked Bob.

'That Maud.'

'What Maud?'

'Comes to stop with the Bakers. Auntie or something.'

Bob knew the Bakers. They were an elderly childless couple living in a neat bungalow at the other end of Springbourne. No one knew much about them, and they 'kept themselves to themselves' as the villagers said, usually with approval.

The general feeling was that it was good of them to

33

have young Maud Gordon now and again, to give her
mother a rest. She was a singularly unattractive child
which made their kindness even more laudable. Mrs Baker
and Mrs Gordon, it was understood, had been in service
together and had remained friends.

'Them ducks wants some bread,' yelled Ted, hands
behind his head and legs stretched out in the sunshine.

Maud tossed her head, and then put out her tongue.

'Watch it!' shouted Ted. 'You'll be stuck like it if the
wind changes!'

Bob was a silent admirer of these witticisms from his
hero, but did not attempt to add his share.

Maud squatted down on the board and began to splash
water over the milling crowd of ducks. They quacked and
flapped but did not retreat, still hoping, no doubt, that
food would soon be forthcoming.

'Watch your step, Maudie!' bawled Ted, and at that the girl stood up, slipped on the slimy board and landed with one leg sunk deep into the muddy water and one out-stretched on the duckboard. Her cotton skirt was stained and dripping, and she was gasping with shock.

Bob was half-frightened although he could see that very little had happened to the girl. But Ted put back his head and roared his amusement to the blue sky above.

'That'll learn you,' he wheezed. 'Teasin' them poor birds! Serves you right. Now run home and tell yer auntie. She'll give you what for!'

Maud struggled out of the pond, and stumped furiously past the boys. Her face was scarlet and one shoe squelched as she made for home.

'You wait, Ted Pickett!' she stormed. 'I'll tell on you!'

Mr Willet paused and looked at my kitchen clock.

'Here I sits natterin' on, and I expect I'm keepin' you from somethin'. Ironin' and that, say?'

'Far from it,' I assured him. 'Go on. Did she tell?'

'That she did, the little besom,' said Mr Willet. 'She went straight home, and she knew damn well she'd get into trouble over that mucky frock, so she said Ted Pickett had pushed her in.'

'No!'

'Yes! The little liar! Why, Ted and me hadn't stirred from that bank. It was much too hot to muck about.'

'What happened?'

'Our Maud told the tale all right, tears and all, and Mrs Baker came storming up to the Picketts' place, breathin' fire and brimstone, so poor old Ted was sent upstairs to wait for his Dad to come home and use his belt.'

'Ted wasn't believed?'

'No. And I didn't know until the next day when Ted showed me his behind – begging your pardon, miss.'

I assured him that I was not shocked.

'And even if I had stuck up for Ted that afternoon, I don't suppose them Picketts would have believed me. After all, boys hangs together at times like that. No, poor old Ted fairly copped it, and all through our Mrs Pringle. Ted's dad was a hefty bloke, and when he used the strap you knew it all right.'

Mr Willet sighed heavily at things remembered, and got to his feet.

'Poor old Ted,' he repeated. 'We stayed friends right up to the outbreak of war, though my old ma never really approved. We joined up the same day in Caxley, but Ted never got back from Dunkirk.'

'That's a sad ending.'

'Sad for both of us,' admitted Bob Willet. 'I always touches his name when I pass the war memorial by the church gate. I miss him still, poor old Ted.'

I accompanied him out of the front door, and thanked him again for the marrows and his story.

'Well, I only told you because I don't want you to worry about Maud Pringle's little ways. She was born a tartar, and she's stayed that way. All Fairacre knows it, so you keep a stout heart.'

I promised that I would, and went back into my house much comforted.

To my secret relief, Mrs Pringle kept the stoves going throughout this unreasonably chilly spell. She even bent so far as to address me now and again, and her leg was not dragged quite so heavily as the days passed. I was not so sanguine as to imagine that all was forgiven, but at least our relationship was civil, if not exactly cordial.

A week or two after our clash over the stoves, Mrs Pringle spoke of Fairacre Women's Institute, and urged me to join.

'It sounds a good idea,' I told her, 'it means that I shall get to know more people.'

'Well, that's a mixed blessing,' was her gloomy reply. 'There's some in this village as should be drummed out, to my way of thinking. Like them Coggses.'

I had heard about Arthur Coggs already, evidently the village ne'er-do-well, and a strong supporter of 'The Beetle and Wedge'. His young and fast-growing family, not to mention his down-trodden wife, went in fear of him. Later I was to have his son Joseph as a pupil.

'But apart from them undesirables,' continued Mrs Pringle, 'there's a lot of good folk you'd like. Mrs Partridge is President. She looks after us a fair treat.'

I could imagine that she would, brave, fair-minded and tactful woman that she was. A vicar's wife must get plenty of day-to-day training in diplomacy.

Consequently, I took myself along to the next meeting and was welcomed with surprising warmth.

We all sang 'Jerusalem' with varied success, listened to interminable arrangements about various activities to which no one apparently wanted to go, and voted on paper for our choice of Christmas treat, Caxley pantomime, tea-party with magician in the village hall, or coach trip to London for Christmas shopping. I plumped for the last, and had visions of going straight to Harrods Food Hall and buying almost all my Christmas presents there in one fell swoop.

After that, a very nervous flower-arranger who was inaudible except to those of us in the front row, showed us how to make 'The Best of our Late Blooms'. The response was lack-lustre, I felt, and only the knitters behind me, busy clicking their needles, really benefitted.

But tea time was the real highlight. Despite the fact that it was past eight o'clock in the evening, we all fell upon home-made sponges, wedges of treacle tart, shortbread fingers, and squares of sticky gingerbread, as though we had not seen food for weeks.

I met a host of cheerful women, several of them with children at the school, and many of them former pupils, and went home as a fully paid-up member of Fairacre's W.I.

It will not surprise any newcomer to a village to know that I was also committed to supplying a contribution to the next month's tea table, and had agreed to stand in for the Treasurer when she had her baby.

Of such stuff is village life made. And very nice, too.

CHAPTER 4

Mrs Willet Goes Farther

One of the nicest women I met at our local Women's Institute was Alice Willet, wife of Bob. She had been at our school as a child, and had many memories of Fairacre folk including Maud Gordon when she visited her adopted uncle and aunt during the school holidays.

'Mind you,' she said, 'I could never take to her. She was a year or two older than me, and bossy with it. I kept out of her way when she was around in Fairacre.'

Some years later, it seems, Miss Parr, who lived at the largest house in Fairacre, was looking for a housemaid to replace her well-trained Mary who had been with her for over twenty years and had had the effrontery to get married.

Miss Parr was a great power in the village. She had, in fact, been the most venerable of the school governors who had appointed me to the headship of Fairacre School, and so I was particularly interested in her history.

Her family, it appears, came from Lancashire where innumerable cotton mills had brought them much wealth in the last century. Hard-headed and shrewd, the money had been invested, not only in enlarging the mills, but in divers other money-making ventures. Miss Parr had inherited a fortune, as well as the commonsense of her forbears, and lived in style in the Queen Anne house in Fairacre.

She employed a head gardener and an under-gardener, and a chauffeur to look after her limousine. Indoors, a cook and a housemaid coped with most of the chores, although a succession of what Miss Parr termed 'village women' came in to help with 'the rough' and the laundry work.

Those she employed spoke well of her, and stayed in her service. She was not lavish in her payments but they were paid on the dot, and in those hard times one was lucky to have a job at all. Also, when the garden was producing more than one lone lady and her staff could consume, the gardeners and the daily helpers could take home this welcome largesse to their families.

'She kept a sharp eye on things, of course,' said Mrs Willet. 'I mean, her people had made their money by looking after the pennies, and she took after them. And when she found old Biddy Stamper had helped herself to a bunch of grapes and some peaches from the hot-house, and was trying to smuggle them out with the washing, she got the sack there and then, and never set foot in the house again.'

Mrs Willet nodded her approval before continuing. 'Well, when Mary left, Mrs Pringle's auntie, Mrs Baker, she went up to Miss Parr's to see if she could put in a word for her Maud. Mrs Baker was one of the women that helped with the ironing each week, so she knew the house and all that. Miss Parr thought a lot of her. She was a dab hand with the ironing, and could use a goffering iron.'

'I've never heard of such a thing!' I exclaimed.

'Oh, it was what you used to crimp the edges of things. Mary's afternoon caps had to be goffered, and some collars

too that she wore. I believe some people even goffered the frills round their pillow cases. Anyway, Mrs Baker was famous for her goffering, and Miss Parr had a soft spot for anyone as was good at their particular job.'

Thus it was that Miss Parr agreed to see Maud, and up the girl went, all dressed neat-but-not-gaudy, to the big house one evening.

'And did she get the job?'

'She did. We was all a bit surprised seeing that Maud was so much younger than Mary, but she'd had a good bit of experience at the Howards' place in Caxley, both in their house and the restaurant, so top and bottom of it was she was taken on.'

'And gave satisfaction obviously.'

'That's right. Well, you know yourself, our Mrs Pringle is a good worker, despite her funny little ways. No one can touch her for cleaning brass, and she can get any bit of furniture up to look like satin. The only snag was Henry.'

'Henry?' I queried.

'The chauffeur. He was a real knock-out. All us girls were a bit soft on Henry.'

Mrs Willet's pale cheeks were suffused with a becoming blush, and her eyes grew misty with memories. Henry, I surmised, must have been a real lady-killer.

'He had dark wavy hair,' continued Mrs Willet, looking dreamily towards the window as if he still lingered in the village outside. 'And one of them Ronald Coleman moustaches. And I've never seen such eye-lashes on anyone, girl or boy. He was nice with it, too. Very soft-spoken, and kind to everyone. Miss Parr thought the world of him, and we did too.'

'Mrs Pringle as well?' I asked, my mind boggling at the thought of Mrs Pringle being undone by love.

'Worse than any of us,' asserted Mrs Willet. 'She was forever making sheep's eyes at him. I was going steady at the time with Bob, so I didn't see a lot of Maud, but all the village was talking about her.'

'What about Henry? It must have been embarrassing for him working at the same place.'

'Nothing worried Henry. He was as nice to Maud as he was to everybody, but he did try and keep out of her way. He didn't want to lose his job after all.'

'Did Miss Parr know?'

'She guessed something was up when she saw Maud coming out of the bothy.'

'The bothy?'

'The room near the coach-house where Henry lived,' explained Mrs Willet. 'Maud had the cheek to take a cake over there for him. Of course, the bothy was out of bounds to women, just as the attics where the maids slept was out of bounds to the men. When Miss Parr caught her, she gave her a fine old dressing-down, but Maud wriggled out of it that time, and was allowed to stay on.'

'She was lucky.'

'But Henry wasn't. Miss Parr had him up in the drawing room that evening and cook heard it all.'

'How?'

'Well, I take it she was passing at the time,' said Mrs Willet, looking slightly confused, 'and then they was both shouting, cook said, so she couldn't help hearing.'

'And what did she hear?'

'Not as much from Miss Parr as she did from Henry, but I gather he fairly let fly when Miss Parr as good as told him that he'd been leading Maud on. "Such a young innocent girl too!" cook heard her say. And evidently that tore it.'

Mrs Willet paused to find a snowy handkerchief in her sleeve. 'He told Miss Parr it was the other way round. Maud had been pestering him. And then he went on to say what he thought of Maud, in the most dreadful language that I wouldn't repeat to you, though cook never turned a hair when she repeated it to all and sundry in Fairacre. My Bob told her to wash out her mouth with carbolic, I remember.'

'So Henry was sacked?'

'No. He gave in his notice there and then, and left at the end of the week. I think Miss Parr regretted the whole affair, but of course it was easier to get a good chauffeur than a good worker like Maud in those days. But how we all missed him!'

Mrs Willet sighed. 'He had a green uniform to match the car. Very trim figure he was in that. What with his smile and his nice ways, he was a real gentleman.'

'What happened to him?'

'He got a job in foreign parts.'

I imagined that trim green-suited figure driving wealthy Americans about, or being snapped up by an Indian rajah.

'Northampton, I think it was,' said Mrs Willet, 'or maybe Leicester. We never saw him again.'

She sounded wistful.

'And Mrs Pringle?'

'Well, with Henry gone she turned her attention to the next best thing on the premises, and that was the under-gardener.'

'What about the head gardener?'

'He was married already, but the under one was easy game. And anyway the head gardener moved off soon after Henry to open a nursery garden of his own, so the under-gardener was promoted and had a rise in wages.'

'How did he respond to Maud's advances?'

'Didn't stand a chance. It was Fred Pringle, you see. He soon knuckled under, and he's stayed that way ever since.'

It was a few days later that Bob Willet continued this enthralling episode in Fairacre's history.

'You could've knocked us down with a feather when we heard poor old Fred was engaged to Maud. Not that he had a chance, of course, but Maud was so high and mighty and the Pringles had a bad name.'

'Why?'

'They was all a bit harum-scarum, and Josh Pringle, Fred's brother, was a proper bad lot – poachin', pinchin', fightin' – always in trouble and turnin' up in Caxley court. No end of kids, and half of them not his wife's, if you follow me.'

I said I did.

'The Bakers was upset about it, but couldn't do much. After all, Maud was of age – *over* age, come to that – and she and Fred got married in Caxley where her parents lived, so us Fairacre folk didn't see or hear much about the weddin'. All this was before the war, of course.'

'But I take it they came to live in Fairacre?'

'Oh yes! In one of Miss Parr's cottages, near where they are now. Fred did the garden and Maud helped in the house until John was on the way when she stopped workin' at Miss Parr's. She used to give a hand once a week to the Hopes who were livin' here at the school house, and then the Bensons when Mr Benson took over. That's when she became school cleaner.'

Mr Willet paused, blowing out his cheeks. 'Still,' he went on, rallying slightly, 'I suppose she's done a good job, considerin'. She done it all through the war, while Fred was away. We all reckoned it did poor old Fred a power of good to get away from Maud during the war. He looked much fresher when he come back.'

'I haven't seen Mr Pringle yet.'

'Nor likely to,' responded Bob Willet. 'After the war he got a job up the Atomic, and he's still at it. Gets the Atomic bus soon after seven, and when he gets home he spends most of the time in that shed of his at the end of the garden.'

'What does he do there?'

'Keeps out of her ladyship's way, I shouldn't wonder, but he makes things with matchsticks as well.'

'Matchsticks?' I exclaimed, my mind boggling.

'Models and that. Fairacre Church he done once, and it was on show at the village fête. Then he done a piano – not life size, of course – and that was a real masterpiece, and a

45

set of chairs for a dolls' house. He's a clever chap in his way, although he don't say much. Come to think of it, I suppose he can't get a word in edgeways with his missus, so he's driven to matchsticks.'

He made for the door. 'Best have another tidy up of the coke pile. Them little varmints can't leave well alone.'

And he departed, leaving me to mull over the story of Mrs Pringle's love life.

During these early days at Fairacre I had a great deal to learn, not only about my new job, but also about the people of the village.

Mrs Pringle herself enlightened me on many aspects of life in the country. At that time the village had no piped water, and rain barrels stood by the houses collecting rainwater from the roofs.

I soon learnt to appreciate this precious fluid, and Mrs Pringle was my chief adviser. What she called 'the top quality', that is the filtered water which supplied the school house, was used for drinking and cooking. The rainwater from the barrels was used for bathing, hair washing, laundering and other household activities, but still had other uses which Mrs Pringle explained to me.

'The soapy water from the washing does for the floors,' she told me, 'and then after that you can use some for pouring over the flagstones on the path, and give them a good brushing with a stiff broom. And what's left you throws over the cabbages and such-like in the garden. There's no need,' she continued, turning a fierce eye upon me, 'to waste a drop!'

In times of drought the villagers were hard-pressed, and Fairacre pond furnished a few precious bucketfuls for cleaning operations. Mr Roberts, the local farmer, had put in a bore to keep his cattle watered, and he let each household have a bucket or two of fresh water from this well for drinking when things became serious.

Of necessity we had earth closets, and thanks to Bob Willet and Mrs Pringle these were kept as hygienic as such primitive amenities could be, but it was a great relief to everyone when water was piped to the village some years after my arrival.

Even so, the old ways persisted, and I noticed that Mrs Pringle transferred what she termed 'lovely suds' from the new wash basins to a pail, in readiness to wash over the lobby floor.

Considering the somewhat primitive hygiene which the Fairacre folk had perforce to endure, it was surprising to see what a healthy lot we all were.

I suppose the air had something to do with it. Even on a still summer's day there is a freshness in this downland air, and in the winter the winds can be ferocious, blowing away not only cobwebs but any germs hovering about, I suspect.

Doctor Martin, who looks after the local population, does not get called upon unnecessarily. Accidents on the farms, unlucky tractor drivers pinned beneath overturned vehicles, men carelessly wielding scythes, hedge slashers and other dangerous implements may get Doctor Martin's ready attention, but minor ailments are usually dealt with at home.

Some of these remedies sound horrific, and over the years Mrs Pringle has curdled my blood with her first-aid tips.

'My young nephew,' she told me once, 'had the whooping cough something dreadful. Nearly coughed his heart up, and Doctor's medicine never done him a bit of good.

In the end, it was Bob Willet's old mother as suggested the fried mouse.'

'Fried mouse?' I quavered.

'Oh, it's a good old cure, is fried mouse. You want a *fresh* one, of course. And it's best to skin it, and then try and eat it whole.'

I must have looked as horrified as I felt.

'It does sound *unpleasant*, don't it?' said Mrs Pringle, with evident satisfaction. 'But no end of people swear by it.'

'Did it help your nephew?'

'Well, no, it didn't seem to work with him, but old Mrs Willet's cure for chilblains was always a winner.'

'And what was that?'

'A thorough thrashing with stinging nettles. Worked like a charm. Always.'

Pondering on this, after Mrs Pringle had left to resume her duties, I could only suppose that the stings from the nettles acted as a counter-irritant to the itching of the chilblains, but it all seemed unnecessarily violent to me, and I resolved to treat any chilblains I might suffer with more orthodox methods.

But in my early days at the school, I soon discovered that apart from the inevitable childish complaints such as measles and chickenpox, my thirty-odd pupils were a hardy lot, only succumbing occasionally to a bout of toothache or earache, or an upset tummy, the latter usually in August or September when the apples and plums were unripe.

The first-aid box, on the wall above the map cupboard, was seldom used; a bottle of disinfectant, lint and bandages for scraped knees and cut fingers were the things most often in demand and, as I pointed out, if the children kept off the coke pile half the injuries would never occur at all.

But I might just as well have saved my breath.

*

It was Mrs Pringle who first pointed out to me that it was traditional at Fairacre School to give a Christmas party to parents and friends.

'I thought as how it should be *mentioned*,' she told me, 'so's you can decide if you want to go on with it. Alice Willet usually bakes a cake – and very nice it is too,' she added graciously.

I said that I thought it was an excellent idea and would start planning straightaway.

Miss Clare confirmed Mrs Pringle's information, and was slightly amused at her early pronouncement.

'I meant to tell you in good time,' she said, 'but Mrs P. has got there first.'

I was careful to find out how things were traditionally done. One has to tread warily in a village, particularly if one is a newcomer. Mrs Willet, it seemed, had the largest square baking tin in the village, and was adept at producing enormous square cakes, ideal for cutting into neat fingers on festive occasions.

'Her coronation cake,' Mrs Pringle told me, 'was a real masterpiece, with a Union Jack piped on it in icing. And *waving* at that!'

It was Miss Clare who told me that it was right and proper for Mrs Willet to be given the ingredients for such an expensive product, but this had to be done with great diplomacy, and the money was usually taken from the school funds.

I negotiated these perils as well as I could, and rather dreaded my meeting with Alice Willet to arrange about making the cake, but my fears were groundless.

One misty November day I called at her cottage after school to broach the subject, but she greeted me with a smile.

'The cake? Why, I made it nearly a month ago. It's not iced yet, of course, but the cake itself needs a few weeks to mature nicely. I always put a spoonful of brandy in it, but I don't tell Bob. He's a strict teetotaller, you see. I don't drink either, but I think a spot of brandy in a good fruit cake, a little drop of sherry in a trifle, makes all the difference.'

I began to make a halting speech about the cost of the cake, and Mrs Willet opened a corner cupboard and took out a neat list which she handed me. It showed all the ingredients and the prices, and the total was shown clearly between two neatly-ruled lines. It seemed extraordinarily modest to me.

I studied the list again.

'But you haven't put in eggs,' I said, feeling rather proud of my perspicacity.

Mrs Willet looked shocked. 'Oh, I wouldn't dream of charging for the eggs! They come from our own chickens, you see.'

'But all the more reason why you should charge for such a first-class product.'

'No, no. I've never done that in all these years. Call it my contribution to Christmas, if you like.'

And with that I had to be content.

The Christmas party took place during the last week of term. The school room was garlanded with home-made paper chains, and a Christmas tree glittered in the corner.

The children acted as hosts to their parents and friends of the school, the stoves roared merrily, and Mrs Willet's Christmas cake was the centre piece of the long tea table. In its centre stood a snowman, some over-large robins and a tiny Christmas tree, and the children were loud in their admiration of Mrs Willet's handiwork.

Among our visitors was Amy, who was quite the most elegant figure among us, and also one of the most appreciative.

At the end of the proceedings, when we had waved goodbye to the children and their guests, we turned back into the quiet school room, crumbs and chaos about us, but also a blessed silence after the junketings.

'Well,' said Amy, 'I don't know when I have enjoyed a party more. You certainly know how to do things in Fairacre.'

I was just beginning to glow with pride at these kind words when the door was flung open and Mrs Pringle stood there surveying the scene.

'Humph!' said the lady, 'about time I made a start, I can see.'

Suddenly chilled, Amy and I made our escape to the school house.

CHAPTER 5

Wartime Memories

As time passed, Mrs Pringle and I established a precari-ous truce. Every now and again she would broach the question of cleaning my house, but I resisted her offers as civilly as I could. Mrs Pringle during school hours was quite enough for me. I hoped that I could keep my home out of that lady's clutches.

There were occasional clashes, of course, and after each one Mrs Pringle's combustible leg would 'flare up', and oblige her to drag the suffering limb about her duties with many a sigh and a wince. I grew very skilled at ignoring these manifestations of Mrs Pringle's umbrage.

The stoves were the usual source of trouble. For some reason, pencil sharpenings near these monsters, usually inside their fireguards, were a major source of irritation. The milk saucepan sometimes left a ring on the jet-black surface, and this too caused sharp comment.

Wet footmarks, coke crunched in, bubble gum, crumbs from lunch packets and any other hazards to Mrs Pringle's floors were also severely criticised and, up to a point, she had my support.

She was indeed a sore trial, but I reminded myself that

she was a superb cleaner, as I was always being told, and that Fairacre School was a model of hygiene in the area.

I also remembered Mr Willet's advice. 'You don't want to worry about her funny ways. She's always been a tartar since a girl. All Fairacre knows that.'

It was some comfort in times of crisis.

Mrs Pringle's bossiness had been well to the fore during the war years it seems. Fairacre, in company with most rural communities, had its fair share of evacuees, and Mrs Pringle was lucky in that the couple billeted upon her were a middle-aged self-effacing pair who inhabited one room of her semi-detached cottage, and who were careful to creep into the kitchen when Mrs Pringle had finished her labours there.

Next door there lived a middle-aged lady, Jane Morgan, who was not as fortunate as Mrs Pringle in her evacuees, Mrs Jarman and her four boisterous children.

They ruled the roost, and soon clashed with Mrs Pringle next door. At the time, Jane Morgan's husband and Fred Pringle were both away in the army. Mrs Jarman's husband had been killed in the blitz of May 1941. It was then that the three solitary women, the four Jarman children, and Mrs Pringle's schoolboy son John were fated to meet at close quarters.

The Jarman family was an indomitable one. Despite the loss of a husband and father, not to mention their home and all that was in it, the Jarmans' cockney spirit remained irrepressible. The children took to taunting Mrs Pringle over the hedge, and when that lady reported the matter to their mother, Mrs Jarman joined battle with equal zest. For once, it seemed, Mrs Pringle was on the losing side.

One of their skirmishes took place in the village hall.

During wartime this building was in constant use for a great many village functions, and also as an extra classroom on weekdays to accommodate the London children evacuated to Fairacre.

It was on the occasion of a local jumble sale that the clash between Mrs Pringle and Mrs Jarman was observed by some dozen or so Fairacre ladies who were sorting out the contributions ready for the Saturday afternoon sale.

Mrs Jarman and Mrs Pringle had entered the hall together. Mrs Pringle deposited a large bundle on the floor before making her way with ponderous dignity to her stall, marked 'Junk', and starting to arrange chipped vases, moulting cushions, lidless saucepans and innumerable objects of china or tarnished metal to which no one could give a name.

Meanwhile, Mrs Jarman had fallen to her knees beside the bundle dropped by her neighbour, and was holding up threadbare underpants, cardigans washed so often that they resembled felt, and a number of men's shirts. She kept up a running commentary as she sorted out the garments. Some of the comments were ribald enough to shock a few of the Fairacre folk, but on the whole there was secret delight in seeing Mrs Pringle discomfited.

'Look at these then!' shrieked Mrs Jarman, scrabbling among the shirts. 'Not a button between them. Who's pinched them, eh?'

Mrs Pringle's voice boomed from her corner. 'I cut them off to use again, as any one would in wartime. There's such a thing as *thrift* which a lot of people not a hundred miles from here don't ever seem to have heard of!'

This lofty speech did nothing to curb Mrs Jarman's spirit.

'How mean can you get!' she yelled back.

'Nothing *mean* about it,' returned Mrs Pringle, putting a

headless garden gnome to best advantage on the stall. 'I simply collect shirt buttons. They're bound to be needed.'

'I'll remember that,' cried Mrs Jarman, unearthing a moth-eaten strip of fur. 'Ah, I wonder what sort of skin disease this ratty old collar would give you!'

'Now that's enough,' said Mrs Partridge, the vicar's wife, who had just arrived. 'Time's getting short, and we must get on.'

Even Mrs Jarman took some notice of Mrs Partridge, and curbed her tongue. Work continued apace, with considerably more decorum, and all the stalls were ready by half past twelve.

The helpers returned to their homes to dish up spam, whale meat, a piece of unidentifiable fish or some other wartime delicacy, before returning to the fray at two-thirty.

*

The open warfare between Mrs Jarman and Mrs Pringle was a source of much pleasure to all who witnessed it, and each skirmish was noted with interest.

It was generally felt that the Battle of the Buttons would have some repercussions, probably on that same day, but there was no sign of anything other than disdain on Mrs Pringle's side and raucous laughter on Mrs Jarman's. Both ladies, in any case, were kept busy with the throng of customers snapping up old shoes, stained waistcoats and cracked crockery throughout the afternoon. Those who had witnessed the earlier exchange were slightly disappointed.

Over the months the shirt button incident was forgotten, and it was not until after Christmas that the sequel to the quarrel became general knowledge in Fairacre.

One of the uses to which the village hall's large copper was put during war time was the communal boiling of the village's Christmas puddings. Each basin was clearly labelled with its owner's name, and all were lodged securely in the capacious boiler.

Naturally, the water had to be topped up at intervals, and a list of ladies was pinned up on the wall. The afternoon session was designated thus:

2.30   Mrs Pringle
3.30   Miss Parr (only that would really be her maid carrying out her elderly mistress's orders)
4.30   Mrs Jarman
5.30   Everyone welcome

This was when the puddings would be claimed by their owners, the boiler turned off, and the village hall locked for the night. The precious puddings, of course, were then carefully stored away in Fairacre larders to await Christmas Day.

It was innocent little Mrs Morgan, unwilling hostess to the Jarman family, who spread the news of Mrs Pringle's remarkable Christmas pudding about the village of Fair-acre.

It so happened that Mrs Pringle had invited her sister and niece to share the Christmas festivities with her son John and herself. Corporal Fred Pringle was on military duty, and so was Jane Morgan's husband.

The Jarmans had invited a horde of relatives and friends to spend the day with them, and Mrs Pringle, prompted more by malice against the Jarmans rather than neighbour-liness to Jane Morgan, hastened to invite that lady to share their Christmas dinner. As Jane and Mrs Pringle's sister were old friends, the invitation was gratefully accepted.

The roast duck was delicious, the vegetables beautifully cooked, and everyone was most complimentary.

The Christmas pudding, steaming and aromatic, awaited Mrs Pringle's knife. It was apparent, as soon as the first slice was removed, that a number of foreign bodies mingled with the glutinous mixture.

'Threepenny bits!' shouted John.

'Sixpences!' squeaked his cousin excitedly.

Mrs Pringle's bewilderment was apparent. 'I don't hold with metal objects in a pudding,' she said austerely, passing plates.

'Quite right,' agreed Jane. 'My mother always said the same, but she did put little china dolls in when we were small. We used to wash them afterwards and put them in the dolls' house.'

But no one was listening to her reminiscences. Forks and spoons were busy pushing the pudding this way and that, and on the rim of each plate a pile of assorted shirt buttons grew larger.

'*Someone*,' said Mrs Pringle with a face like thunder, 'has been playing tricks on us, and I know just who it is!'

At that moment, a particularly loud yell of half-tipsy laughter could be heard through the wall.

Mrs Pringle rose majestically and went to open the last precious tin of pineapple chunks to augment the despoiled Christmas pudding.

Boxing Day had hardly passed before the sequel to the Battle of the Buttons was known to all Fairacre. But Mrs Jarman denied any knowledge of it.

It was Mrs Willet who told me this tale. She and many other Fairacre folk had happy memories of the evacuees, and the relationship was kept fresh by an annual reunion in our village hall each summer.

Soon after I had settled in Fairacre, I was invited to help in getting preparations ready for the visitors. As you can imagine, I looked out for Mrs Jarman, and there she was, a little sharp-faced woman with unnaturally blonde hair and lots of make-up. Her shrill laugh rang out over the general hubbub, and I saw Mrs Pringle sail by with face averted. Mrs Jarman made some comment which was greeted with half-scandalised tittering from the cronies around her. Could it have been some quip about shirt buttons, I wondered?

I could quite understand the affection which had grown up between our country women and their town guests during the dark days of war. Mrs Jarman epitomised the cockney effervescence which had survived the blitz, and defied threats and even death itself.

Mrs Willet and I walked home together when the party was over and our visitors had boarded their coaches.

Mrs Willet spoke wistfully. 'I always liked those Londoners. They were a real larky lot!'

I had just arrived home, and was sitting on the couch with my feet up, wondering if I had the strength to switch on the kettle after my labours, when Amy arrived looking as chic as ever.

'You look terrible,' she said in that downright tone old friends use when making wounding remarks. 'Honestly, you look ten years older than when I saw you last.'

'So would you,' I retorted, 'if you had spent the day coping with evacuees.'

'Good grief! Don't say another war's started!'

'No, just a hang-over from the last,' and I went on to explain.

'I expect you'd like a cup of tea,' I added, suddenly remembering my duties as hostess, and wondering if I could ever move from the couch.

'Well . . .' began Amy, and then stopped as I began to laugh. 'What's the joke?'

'Do you remember a wartime cartoon in *Punch*? The hostess is saying: "If you *do* take milk in your tea, it is absolutely no bother for me to get out my bike and cycle three miles to the farm." Well, I feel a bit like that.'

'I'll put on the kettle,' said Amy kindly, and went to do so.

I stirred myself to follow her after a few minutes, and found her peering into three tins, each containing tea.

'Which do I use? You really should have these labelled, you know.'

'Well, *I* know which is which, so it would be a waste of time and labels. That blue one has Earl Grey, the red one holds Indian, and the black one has Darjeeling in it – I think, but I'm not sure, so I hardly ever use it. Anyway it takes ages to get to the right colour.'

'You really are hopelessly disorganised,' said Amy, spooning Indian tea into the teapot. 'I'll write you three labels myself when we've had this.'

'Wicked waste of paper,' I told her, 'cutting down all those forests to make labels.'

We carried our mugs into the sitting room and smiled at each other over the steam.

'How's James?' I asked.

'Off to Amsterdam at the end of the week.'

'He might bring you back some diamonds,' I said.

'An Edam cheese, more likely,' responded Amy. 'He can eat it by the pound, but I find it too rubbery.'

She began to look about her in an enquiring way. 'Have you got a mat, or a tile, or something for me to put this hot mug on? I don't like standing it on the table. Even yours,' she added unnecessarily.

'Oh, don't be so fussy!' I retorted. 'Bung it down on the corner of the newspaper.'

'Well, it may mark the television programmes for this evening, but I don't suppose that's any great loss. I pine to have a play about ordinary normal people instead of all these programmes about unfortunates who can't see, or can't hear, or have other disabilities.'

'I know. I'm getting tired too of having my withers wrung every time I switch on. If it isn't flood or famine, it's more sophisticated ways of killing each other.'

Amy moved her mug to the edge of the newspaper and studied the evening's offerings.

'There's an hour of medical horrors, including a blow-by-blow, or perhaps cut-by-cut might be a better description, of a hip replacement operation. On another channel there's a jolly half-hour entitled "How to Succeed despite Degenerative Diseases", and there's a discussion on the radio about "The Horrors of our Geriatric Wards"!'

'Mrs Pringle should be all right tonight then,' I said. 'She told me she loves a good operation on the telly.'

61

'And how is the lady? Is her leg still in a state of spontaneous combustion?'

'It's fairly quiescent at the moment, although she did roll down her stocking yesterday, when the children were out in the playground, to show me her varicose veins.'

'I hope you studied them with due reverence.'

'One glance was more than enough,' I confessed. 'I think she thought me very callous not to spend longer poring over them. Her parting shot was to the effect that Veins Come To Us All, and that my time would soon come.'

'Ah well,' said Amy, 'she may be right at that. Now, are you going to let me label those tea tins before I go?'

'No, Amy dear. I'll just muddle along as usual.'

'You know,' she remarked, flicking a dead leaf from the window sill, 'having Mrs Pringle once a week might be a good thing in this place. Why don't you think about it?'

'I have. Nothing doing. You know yourself what a pain in the neck she is.'

'Yes, but sometimes this house . . .' She let her voice trail away into something like despair.

I put my arm comfortingly round her shoulders as we went out to the car. 'Don't worry about me. I'm managing perfectly well on my own,' I told her.

Later I was to remember this conversation.

As time passed I began to realise that Mrs Pringle was slightly more approachable during the summer months than the winter ones. I put this down to the fact that her cleaning duties were considerably lighter. For one thing, the treasured stoves were not in use, and so less mess was caused by the carrying of coke to and fro.

Naturally, a certain amount was scrunched into the school floor-boards by miscreants who had disobeyed rules and had run up and down the coke pile in the playground. Mrs Pringle's eagle eye soon noticed any traces of the offending fuel and complained bitterly.

I sometimes thought too that she missed her cosseting of the stoves during the summer months. A flick with a duster night and morning was all that was needed, and it seemed to me that, in some perverse way, she regretted the ministrations with blacklead and brush which dominated the winter months.

Nevertheless, on the whole, she appeared marginally more cheerful in the summer. The light evenings gave her more scope in arranging her cleaning activities, and I frequently heard her singing some lugubrious hymn as she went about her work when I was in the garden after school hours.

It so happened that one particular April was unseasonably warm, and I decreed that the stoves could be allowed to go out.

'Well, I'm not arguing about that,' said Mrs Pringle. 'Dear knows I've got enough to do in this place, and it'll be a treat not to have coke all over the floor.'

She walked quite briskly about the classroom, dusting energetically without a trace of a limp, before the children came into morning prayers.

'I'll put the stoves to rights this evening,' she told me as she departed. 'See you midday.'

She always returned in the early afternoon to wash up the school dinner things. Usually our paths did not cross then, for I was teaching and she was alone in the lobby.

On this particular day I heard her at her labours. At the same time, the bell of St Patrick's church next door began to toll. The children looked up from their work and there was some whispering.

I went out to the lobby to see if Mrs Pringle could

enlighten me. Obviously, someone of local importance had died. Mrs Pringle was standing in the steamy lobby, her hands red and puffy from her task. To my amazement she was trembling and there were tears in her eyes.

'It's Miss Parr,' she said, before I could make any enquiry, 'went sudden about five this morning.'

'It has upset you,' I replied, as much in wonderment as in sympathy. This was the first time I had seen Mrs Pringle in a weak condition. I was much moved.

'She was good to me. I was in service with her before I married.'

'I did know that.'

'Gave me this and that quite frequent, but that weren't all.'

'What else?'

'She took my word against others when I was in trouble once. I never forgot that. I might have lost my job, but she stood by me.'

Two tears rolled down her cheeks, and I found myself patting her substantial shoulder.

'Well, this won't do,' she said, sniffing loudly, 'can't bring back the dead, can you? Best get on with my job.'

She sounded much more like her tough old self, and I left her smoothing the tea towels over the still-warm boiler to dry.

But I noticed that her puffy hands still trembled.

Later that evening I pondered over this surprising episode. I remembered Alice Willet's account of the row over the chauffeur and his fierce denial of any interest in the love-lorn Maud, and his consequent departure to foreign parts.

It looked as though Mrs Pringle still had feelings of guilt over her part in the proceedings. Did she regret her

faults as poignantly as she mourned the loss of the dashing
Henry in his bottle-green uniform? And had Fred Pringle,
the next best thing, ever given her any comfort in the years
between?

So much must remain conjecture, but one thing was
certain. Mrs Pringle, my arch enemy, had some human
feelings after all. Those few sad minutes in the steamy
lobby had been a revelation to me, and I felt a new regard
for her.

CHAPTER 6

Joseph Coggs and Mrs Pringle

Every community has its problem families. At Spring-bourne, our neighbouring village, the black sheep was Fred Pringle's brother Josh and his unfortunate relations.

In Fairacre we had the Coggs family. As in the case of Josh Pringle, all blame for the situation lay squarely on the shoulders of Arthur Coggs, the father. By nature he was lazy and of low intelligence. Added to that was his addiction to drink which made him boastful and belligerent when in his cups. It also made him a petty thief for he could not do without his beer, and was very seldom treated; Arthur Coggs, it was soon discovered, never stood his round.

He had various jobs, none of which lasted very long. He occasionally found casual work as a labourer on a building site, or as a roadman for the Caxley council. But absence, arriving late, and taking time off to visit the nearest pub soon ended his employment.

Mr Roberts, the Fairacre farmer, had done his best to give him work. He pitied Arthur's poor down-trodden wife, and the fast-growing family, but Arthur's feckless ways soon exhausted his employer's patience, and apart from a little spasmodic field work at the appropriate time, Mr Roberts could do no more.

The village folk looked upon the Coggses with mingled pity and exasperation.

'If that gel of Arthur's had taken the rolling pin to him early on,' said Mr Willet roundly, 'she'd have done the right thing.'

'But he could easily have killed her,' I cried. 'She's a poor wispy little thing and must be terrified of him.'

'Bullies is always cowards,' replied Mr Willet trenchantly. 'Arthur's got away with it too easy, that's his trouble.'

Naturally, Mrs Pringle was the loudest in her condemnation of the slatternly ways of Mrs Coggs and her husband. As a strict teetotaller she also deplored Arthur's drunken habits.

'I know for a fact he signed the pledge, same as dozens of us years ago. A fat lot of good that done him. He's a proper waster, and we're all sorry for his poor wife. Not that she does much to help herself or that row of kids. She may be short of money, I give you that, but soap and water cost nothing, and those children and the house are a disgrace.'

'She doesn't have much of a chance,' I observed, opening the register and looking pointedly at the wall clock which said ten to nine.

'Those as behaves like doormats,' quoth Mrs Pringle, 'gets treated like 'em!'

As usual, she had the last word, and swept out into the lobby, meeting the rush of children who were swarming into school.

I had been at Fairacre School some five or six years when Joseph Coggs became a pupil. I liked the child from the start. He was dark-haired and dark-skinned, with large mournful eyes. Somewhere in the past there had been gipsy forbears. He was appreciative of all that happened in school, and seemed to settle into an ordered way of life for which his early years could not have trained him.

He was in Miss Clare's class in the infants' room, so that I did not see a great deal of him. But he was an enthusiastic eater, and demolished his plates of school dinner with a joy which I shared whilst watching him.

The Coggs family lived in a broken-down cottage, one of four collectively called Tyler's Row. Their landlord was an old soldier who could not afford to keep the property in good heart, and it was widely thought that it would be better to see the whole place pulled down, and the families rehoused.

Not that all four cottages were as deplorable as the Coggs' establishment. The Waites next door kept their identical accommodation as neat as a new pin. An elderly couple in the first cottage were also house-proud, and Mrs Fowler who lived in the last one, although feared by all for her violent temper, was certainly house-proud to the point of fanaticism.

It was not surprising that the Coggses were a source of trouble to their close neighbours. Arthur Coggs's habit of roaring home when the pubs had closed did not make him popular. The neglected garden sent its weeds into the neighbouring neat plots, and the cries of unhappy children were clearly heard through the thin dividing walls.

'I wouldn't live near them Coggses for a bag of gold,' Mrs Pringle told me. 'They get more help than the rest of the village put together, but what good does that do 'em? All goes down Arthur's throat, that's what!'

As usual, she was right of course. Mrs Partridge, our vicar's wife, had told me of the kindness of people in the village who had provided clothes, bed linen, furniture and even pots and pans for the pathetic family.

'Most of the stuff,' said Mrs Partridge, 'was never seen again. Arthur exchanged all he could with his cronies and put the money on the bar counter. Gerald has taken him to task on many occasions, and I think he tries for a day or two, but soon falls back into his old bad habits. He was put on probation after one court appearance, and things were slightly better when the probation officer kept an eye on the family. But it really is a hopeless task.'

Mrs Pringle's attitude to Joseph Coggs on his arrival as a pupil was one of lofty disdain. Anyone, or anything, as grubby as the little boy was unwelcome. Not that she said anything to hurt the child's feelings, but he was ignored rather pointedly, I considered, and my affection for him was obviously deplored.

Not long after his entry into the school, there was a most disturbing incident. Mr Roberts, the farmer who is also one of Fairacre School's governors, had been missing eggs from the nest-boxes. He suspected that one of the children had been taking them, and very reluctantly asked me if he could look through the pockets of the coats hanging in the lobby.

Poor man! He was most unhappy about it all. We asked the children if they knew anything about it, but there was no response. Consequently, Mr Roberts and I went through their pockets and found three marked eggs in young Eric's pocket.

When faced with this, the boy confessed tearfully that he had indeed been taking the eggs, and on several occasions.

'And I give some to little Joe Coggs,' he sniffled abjectly. 'He saw me, and I never wanted him to tell.'

We dealt with the malefactor fairly leniently as he obviously was suffering much, though not as severely as Mr Roberts himself who was far more agitated than Eric or young Joseph when I confronted the little boy later. He had handed the eggs to his mother, who must have guessed that they were obtained by stealing, but was too delighted with the gift to take the matter further.

Mrs Pringle's attitude to the incident was predictable. 'What do you expect from that lot?' she asked dismissively.

'It won't happen again,' I assured her, 'both boys were very contrite.'

'It's easy enough to be *contrite*, as you call it, when you've been found out. But in my opinion, that Joe wants watching. Them Coggses is all tarred with the same brush.'

All the new entrants settled in quickly that term under Miss Clare's kindly guidance, and Joseph, although not particularly bright academically, proved to be a helpful and happy little boy.

The weather remained quite warm all through September and the early part of October, but suddenly the chill of autumn struck with clammy fog which veiled the downs and misted the school windows.

Our building is old and damp, and the skylight an ever-present trouble to us, admitting rain in wet weather and a howling draught at all times.

'Better start the stoves,' I said to Mrs Pringle, and waited for the usual delaying tactics.

'Bob Willet hasn't done me any kindling wood.'

'I'll see him at dinner time.'

'One of the coke hods is broken at the bottom.'

'I'll indent for another one. You should have told me before.'

'Matches is short, too.'

'I'll bring you a box from the house at play time.'

Then, her final thrust: 'What will The Office say?'

'I can deal with the Office. *Just light the stoves!*'

Mrs Pringle, bristling with umbrage and muttering darkly, left my presence limping heavily.

We needed those stoves in the weeks that followed for winter seemed to have arrived early. A sharp east wind blew away the fog after some days, and draughts whistled round the classrooms. Every time the door opened, papers fluttered to the floor and top-heavy vases, stuffed with branches of autumn foliage, capsized and spilt water, berries and leaves everywhere. It was impossible to dodge the draught from the skylight, and I had a stiff neck only partially eased by a scarf tied round it.

The children wore their winter woollies or dungarees. Summer sandals were exchanged for wellingtons or stout shoes. The shabbiest of all the children was Joseph, but even he had an extra cardigan – once owned by a girl if the buttoning was anything to go by – and I noticed that Miss Clare had moved him to a desk close to the stove.

The infants went home a quarter of an hour earlier than my class, but on one particularly bitter afternoon, as I was seeing my children out, I saw that Joseph was still in the playground.

'I was waitin' for Ernest,' he said gruffly in reply to my questioning. 'I goes a bit of the way with him.'

The child's hands were red with the cold, and he was sniffing lustily. I handed him a tissue from my pocket supply.

71

'No gloves?' I asked.

'No, miss.'

At that moment Ernest appeared.

'Well put your hands in your pockets,' I advised, 'and run along together to get warm.'

A few days later I had occasion to go into Miss Clare's classroom. As in my own, a row of damp scarves and gloves steamed gently over the top rail of the fireguard round the tortoise stove. Among the motley collection was a pair of thick red woollen gloves, obviously expertly knitted in double-knitting wool. I turned them over to help the drying process.

Joseph, from his nearby desk, looked up with pride. 'They's mine,' he said, 'Mrs Pringle give 'em to me.'

I exchanged puzzled glances with Miss Clare.

72

'I'll tell you later,' she whispered.

It all happened evidently on the afternoon when I had despatched Ernest and Joseph homeward in the bitter cold.

When Ernest had turned into his cottage, not far from the school, Joseph had continued on his solitary way. Most of his schoolfellows had run homeward, keen to get to the fireside and some welcoming food. Joseph, whose home was short of both comforts, dawdled along the village street, occasionally looking through a lighted window for interest.

As he came to the Post Office, which stood back from the village street, he was surprised, and a little alarmed, to hear a shout from Mr Lamb standing in his doorway.

'Joe! Come here a minute, boy.'

Wondering if he had done anything wrong, Joe approached. Grown-ups meant authority, and young Joseph was wary of tangling with those in power, used as he was to his parents' attitude to the police, the probation officer and even the kindly vicar himself.

Mr Lamb, unaware of the trepidation in young Joe's heart, was holding out a large door key.

'Can you nip round to Mrs Pringle's, Joe? She left the school key here when she dropped in for some stamps just now. She'll need it to get in for her cleaning any time now.'

Joseph, much relieved, and somewhat flattered to be entrusted with this task, nodded his assent and Mr Lamb put the heavy key into the small cold palm, folding the fingers over it.

'Don't drop it, will you? Be a fine old to-do if that got lost. I can't leave the shop, or I'd pop down myself, but it's not much beyond your place.'

73

'That's all right,' replied Joseph, and set off, clutching his burden.

His trepidation returned when he got to Mrs Pringle's back door. No one in his station of life would dare to knock at the front one, and Joseph automatically trotted round to the rear door, knocked timidly, and waited.

Mrs Pringle, who had seen the little figure coming up the path, appeared in the doorway Mutely, Joseph held out the key. Here was authority at its most formidable, and the child was struck dumb.

'Well, I'm blowed!' said Mrs Pringle, dignity abandoned in her shock. 'Where did you get that, Joe?'

'Mr Lamb,' faltered Joseph. 'You left it in the Post Office.'

'I've been looking all over for it,' said Mrs Pringle, 'and been worrying about where it could be. Been through my oil-cloth bag times without number, and was just going to search the street.'

She took the key from the child's hand, and felt how cold it was, as cold as the heavy key itself.

'Where's your gloves, boy?'

'Ain't got none.'

'Not at home even?'

'No.'

Mrs Pringle snorted, and Joseph felt his fear returning. Was it so wrong not to have gloves?

'Well, you're a good boy to have brought my key back. You run along home now before it gets dark, and thank you.'

The child turned without a word, cold hands thrust into the pockets of his dilapidated raincoat, and made his way homeward.

*

Later in the day when I had first seen Joe's new gloves, Mrs Pringle and I were alone in the classroom. The children had gone home and all was quiet.

I locked my desk drawers while Mrs Pringle dusted window sills and hummed 'Lead kindly light, amidst the encircling gloom', rather flat.

The key in my hand reminded me of Joseph Coggs. Curiosity prompted me to broach the subject.

'Young Joe has a splendid pair of winter gloves,' I observed.

The humming stopped, and Mrs Pringle faced me, looking disconcerted, which was a rare occurrence.

'Well, time he had! No child should be out in this weather with his hands bare.'

'No,' I agreed. She was about to resume her dusting, but I wanted to know more.

'And were you the kind soul who knitted them?'

Mrs Pringle sat heavily on a desk which creaked in protest.

'The child did me a good turn,' she said. 'I been and left the school key on Mr Lamb's counter, and he give it to Joe to bring along to me. And that child's hands!'

Here Mrs Pringle raised her own podgy ones in horror. 'Cold as clams, they was. A perishing day it was, as well I know, having to get these stoves going far too early. I don't hold with encouraging them Coggses in their slatternly ways, but there's such a thing as Christian Kindness, and seeing how young Joe had helped me out, I thought: "One good turn deserves another" and I got down to the knitting that same evening.'

'It was very good of you,' I said sincerely.

'Well, I had a bit of double-knitting over from our John's sweater, and it did just nicely. The boy seemed grateful. I slipped them to him a morning or two later, and told him to keep them out of his dad's sight.'

'Surely he wouldn't take those?'

'Arthur Coggs,' said Mrs Pringle, 'would drink the coat off your back, if you gave him a chance. And now, if I don't get this dusting done I shan't be back in time to get Pringle's tea.'

Thus dismissed, I left her to her cleaning. She was still humming as I closed the door – it sounded like 'Abide with me', rather sharp.

Whether it was the inescapable draught from the skylight, the wintry weather, or simply what the medical profession calls 'a virus' these days, the result was the same. I went down with an appalling cold.

It was one of those which cannot be ignored. For

several days I had been at the tickly throat stage with an occasional polite blow into a handkerchief, but one night, soon after my conversation with Mrs Pringle, all the germs rose up in a body and attacked me.

By morning every joint ached, eyes streamed, head throbbed and I was too cowardly to take my temperature. It was quite clear that I should be unable to go over to the school, for as well as being highly infectious and pretty useless, I was what Mr Willet described once as 'giddy as a whelk'.

I scribbled a note to Miss Clare, and dropped it from my bedroom window to the first responsible child to appear in the playground.

At twenty to nine, my gallant assistant appeared at the bedroom door.

'Don't come any nearer,' I croaked. 'I'm absolutely leprous. I'm so sorry about this. As soon as it is nine o'clock I'll ring the Office and see if we can get a supply teacher for a couple of days.'

'I shall ring the Office,' said Miss Clare, with great authority, 'and I shall bring you a cup of tea and some aspirins, and see that Doctor Martin calls.'

I was too weak to argue and accepted her help gratefully.

After my cup of tea I must have fallen asleep, for the next I knew was the sound of Doctor Martin's voice as he came upstairs. As always, he was cheerful, practical and brooked no argument.

'When did this start?' he asked when he had put the thermometer into my mouth.

I wondered, not for the first time, why doctors and dentists ask questions when you are effectively gagged by the tools of their trade.

77

'About two or three days ago,' I replied, when released from the thermometer.

'You should have called me then,' he said severely. How is it, I wondered, that doctors can so quickly put you in the wrong?

Relenting, he patted my shoulder. 'You'll do. I'll just write you a prescription and you are to stay in bed until I come again.'

'And when will that be?' I asked, much alarmed.

'The day after tomorrow. But I shan't let you loose until that temperature's gone down.'

He collected his bits and pieces, gave me a beaming smile, and vanished.

I resumed my interrupted slumbers.

It was getting dark when I awoke, and I could hear the children running across the playground on their way home. I could also hear movements downstairs, and wondered if Miss Clare had come over again on a mission of mercy, but to my surprise, it was Amy who appeared, bearing a tea tray.

I struggled up, wheezing a welcome.

'Dolly Clare rang me,' she said, 'and as James is in Budapest, or it may be Bucharest, I was delighted to come. What's more, I've collected your prescription, and pretty dire it looks and smells.'

She deposited a bottle of dark brown liquid on the bedside table.

'I may not need it,' I said, 'after a good cup of tea.'

'You'll do as you're told,' replied Amy firmly, 'and take your nice medicine as Doctor Martin said.'

We sipped our tea in amicable silence, and then Amy told me that she intended to stay until the doctor called again.

'But what about the school? I can't leave Miss Clare to cope alone.'

'Someone's coming out tomorrow, I gather, and in any case, I could do a hand's turn. I *am* a trained teacher, if you remember, and did rather better than you did in our final grades.'

She vanished to make up the spare bed, and left me to my muddled thoughts for some time. I thought I heard her talking outside in the playground. but decided it must be Miss Clare or even Mrs Pringle going about their affairs.

When Amy reappeared, the clock said half past seven.

'I can't think what's happened to today,' I complained, 'I must keep falling asleep.'

'You do,' she assured me, 'and a good thing too.'

'But there's such a lot to do. The kitchen's in a fine mess. I left yesterday's washing up, and the grate hasn't been cleared.'

'Oh yes, it has! Mrs Pringle came over after she'd finished at the school. She had it all spick and span in half an hour.'

'Amy,' I squeaked, 'you haven't asked *Mrs Pringle* to help! You know how I've resisted all this time.'

'And what's more,' went on Amy imperturbably, 'she is quite willing to come every Wednesday afternoon, if you need her.'

'Traitor!' I said, but I was secretly amused and relieved.

'Time for medicine,' replied Amy, advancing on the bottle.

CHAPTER 7

Christmas

As so often happens in the wake of nervous apprehension, reality proved less severe than my fears.

The advent of Mrs Pringle into my personal affairs had its advantages. For one thing, the house benefitted immediately from her ministrations. Furniture gleamed like satin, windows were crystal clear, copper and brass objects were dazzling, and even door knobs on cupboards, which had never hitherto seen a spot of Brasso, were transformed.

The beauty of it was, from my point of view, that I hardly came across the lady when she was at her labours. She chose to come on a Wednesday afternoon. (Mrs Hope, that paragon of domestic virtue who had been an earlier occupant in the school house, had always preferred Wednesdays, according to Mrs Pringle.) So Wednesday it was.

She went straight from her washing up in the school lobby to my house, and worked from half past one until four o'clock. As I was teaching then it meant that I seldom saw her in the house, but simply marvelled at the shining surfaces when I returned.

Occasionally, of course, I ran into her and we would share a pot of tea before she set off for home.

It was on one of these tea-drinking sessions that she first told me about her niece, Minnie Pringle, daughter of the black sheep of the family, Josh Pringle of Springbourne.

'She come up this morning to see if I'd got any jumble for their W.I. sale next week. At least, that's what *she said* she'd come for, but it was money she was after for herself.'

I knew that the girl had two small children, so enquired innocently if her husband was out of work.

'*Work?* A *husband?*' cried Mrs Pringle. 'Minnie never had a husband. These two brats of hers is nothing more than you-know-what beginning with a B but I wouldn't soil my lips with saying it.'

'Oh dear,' I said feebly. 'I didn't realise . . .'

'And another on the way, as far as I could see this morning. One is one thing, most people give a girl the benefit of the doubt. But two is taking things too far, especially when the silly girl can't say for sure who the father is.'

'She must have *some* idea.'

'Not Minnie, she's that feckless she just wouldn't remember. Not that she's entirely to blame. That father of hers, our Josh – though I'm ashamed to claim him as part of the Pringle family – he's an out and out waster, and his poor wife is as weak-minded as our Minnie. Nothing but a useless drudge, and never gave Minnie any idea of Right and Wrong.'

'But surely –' I began, but was swept aside by Mrs Pringle's rhetoric. Mrs P. in full spate is unstoppable.

'I told her once, "If you can't tell that girl of yours the facts of life, then send her to church regular. She'll soon find out all about adultery."'

It seemed a somewhat narrow approach to the church's teachings but I did not have the strength to argue.

'More tea?' I asked.

Mrs Pringle raised a massive hand, rather as if she were holding up the traffic. 'Thank you, no. I'm awash. Must get along to fetch my washing in. It looks as though there's rain to come.'

I accompanied her to the gate. A few children were still in the playground taking their time to go home.

'Mind you,' said Mrs Pringle, dropping her voice to a conspiratorial whisper in deference, I presumed, to the innocent ears so near us, 'if there *is* another on the way, I shan't put myself out with more baby knitting. Minnie don't have any idea how to wash knitted things. It's my belief she *boils them*!'

As Christmas approached that term, the school began to deck itself ready for the festival.

In the infants' room a Christmas frieze running around the walls kept Miss Briggs's children busy. Santa Claus, decked in plenty of cotton wool, Christmas trees, reindeer resembling rabbits, otters, large dogs and other denizens of the animal world, as well as sacks of toys, Christmas puddings, Christmas stockings and various other domestic signs of celebration were put in place by the young teacher's careful hands, and glitter was sprayed plentifully at strategic points.

At least, the stuff was supposed to be at strategic points such as the branches of the Christmas trees, but glitter being what it is we found it everywhere. It appeared on the floor, on the window sills, in the cracks of desks, and sometimes a gleam would catch our eyes in the school dinner, blown there, no doubt, by the draught from the door. The stoves suffered too, much to Mrs Pringle's disgust.

In my own room, glitter was banned on the grounds

that we had quite enough from the room next door, but we had a large picture of a Christmas tree, on which the children stuck their own bright paintings. We also made dozens of Christmas cards for home consumption, and some rather tricky boxes to hold sweets.

I bought the sweets, a nice straightforward approach to Christmas jollifications. The construction of the boxes, which appeared such a simple operation from the diagram in *The Teachers' World*, was not so easy. Half the boxes burst open at the seams whilst being stuck together. The rest looked decidedly drunken. By the time we had substituted a household glue for the paste we had so hopefully mixed up, the place reeked with an unpleasant fishy smell and I was apprehensive about the sweets although they were wrapped.

However, nothing could quell the high spirits of the children, and the traditional Christmas party for their parents and friends of the school was its usual jubilant occasion on the last afternoon.

We all wished each other a happy Christmas as our guests made their way out into the December dark. I waved goodbye until the last figure had disappeared, locked the school door upon the chaos within – plentifully besprinkled with glitter – and returned thankfully to the peace of the school house.

Tomorrow, I had told Mrs Pringle, would be soon enough to tackle the clearing up, and I would give her a hand.

Meanwhile, I was content to sit down in my armchair and to let the blessed quietness of my home surround and soothe me.

I slept like a log, and then ate a hearty breakfast, much

cheered by the thought that it was the first day of the holidays.

Amy had invited me to her house at Bent for Christmas, and as it fell conveniently on a Sunday this year I should have a wonderful weekend amidst the luxury of Amy and James's home.

Meanwhile, I remembered my duty to Mrs Pringle, and hurried across the playground to the school to set about taking down the decorations and putting away some of the Christmas pictures.

I half expected to hear Mrs Pringle's morose singing as I approached. Instead, I heard her scolding someone, and thought that she might have surprised a child returning to collect something it had forgotten in the excitement of the Christmas party.

But it was not one of my schoolchildren who was being harangued. A little boy of three or four years was sucking his thumb and gazing at the school cleaner. He did not appear to be at all upset.

'Ah, Miss Read,' cried Mrs Pringle, 'I'm sorry to be burdened with *this*, today of all days, but our Minnie has had to catch the Caxley, and there was only me to mind this 'un.'

'The Caxley' is the term used in our downland villages for either the bus which goes to Caxley, as in this case, or for the local newspaper *The Caxley Chronicle*.

'You must have seen it in the *Caxley*,' we say. 'There was a wedding photo in the *Caxley*,' and so on.

'Our Min's taken the other child to *hospital*,' continued Mrs Pringle, giving full weight and reverence to the last word. 'There was an *accident*!'

'Oh dear! What happened?'

Mrs Pringle eyed the little boy who was idly wiping his wet thumb along the edge of my desk.

'Give over!' bellowed Mrs Pringle, nearly making me jump out of my skin. The child appeared unmoved.

'I'll give him something to do,' I said hastily, always the teacher, and went to the cupboard for paper and crayons. We settled the child in a distant desk, and I prepared to listen to Mrs Pringle's account.

For the sake of appearances I took a few drawing pins out of the pictures pinned to the wooden partition, and dropped them back into their tin.

'That Minnie,' said Mrs Pringle in a wrathful whisper, 'brought these two in first thing this morning with some cock-and-bull story about collecting evergreens and ivy and that for Springbourne church. As if Springbourne hasn't got ivy enough without coming all the way to Fairacre!'

'Quite,' I said.

'Well, I'd just put some dried peas to soak for tomorrow's dinner, and before you could say Jack Robinson that dratted first kid of hers had the bowl over and was fiddling about on the floor, getting in everyone's way as we started to pick up the mess. Then what?'

She stopped dramatically. The silence was split by the sound of an appalling sniff from our visitor. Automatically I handed him a tissue from my permanent store, and returned to Mrs Pringle.

'We'd hardly got the peas back in the bowl and put fresh water on 'em, when that child started grizzling, and fidgeting with his ear-'ole. D'you know what that little varmint had done?'

'Stuffed a pea in his ear,' I said, 'it often happens. With beads too, if they are small enough. And I once had a child push a hazelnut up its nose, from the nature table –'

But my tale was cut short by my fellow storyteller. She disliked having her thunder stolen.

'*One in each ear!*' roared Mrs Pringle. 'And I daresay he would have put more in his nose, and *elsewhere*, if we hadn't caught him. And could we get them out?'

I guessed correctly that this was only a rhetorical question intended to heighten the dramatic effect.

'With them being wet, you see,' resumed the lady, 'they was beginning to plump up – the peas, I mean, not his ears – and we tried everything, fingernails, pen knife, even a skewer –'

I must have shuddered.

'Well, we had to *try*,' said Mrs Pringle grumpily.

'Of course, of course.' I began to roll up a picture of a sleigh pulled by reindeer.

'So I said to Minnie, "It's no good you standing there

hollering. Get on the Caxley with him and cut up to the Casualty. They'll have instruments for getting peas out of ear-'oles." Must be at it daily up there.'

'The best thing,' I agreed, still envisaging a meat skewer being twisted in the child's ear.

'So here I am, ten minutes late, and *hampered*, as you see.'

She cast a malevolent glance at the silent child who was now engrossed in scribbling energetically with his crayons. As far as I could see, he was drawing a tangle of multi-coloured wool, but it kept him quiet.

'I told Minnie I'd keep him till she got back, but there isn't another Fairacre till midday, unless she gets the Beech Green and walks the rest.'

She gave a sigh which rustled the pictures still on the wall. 'Children!' she groaned. 'D'you want them wash basins done too?'

'Yes please,' I said.

She pushed herself up from the desk where she had seated herself during the recital of her woes, and limped towards the lobby.

We continued our labours in silence.

It was good to go to Amy's. Dearly as I love my own home and the village of Fairacre, it is exciting to have a change of scenery and company.

Tibby, my spoilt cat, was in the care of Mr Willet who had promised to come up night and morning to see that all was well.

'Strikes me,' he had said, on being shown the pile of tins left for Tibby's sustenance, 'that that cat of yours eats a damn sight better than we do.'

'Well, it is *Christmas*,' I said weakly.

'I'll bring him up a slice of turkey,' replied Mr Willet, 'or ain't that good enough?'

I was not sure if he were being heavily sarcastic, or meant what he said, so I contented myself with sincere thanks, handing over a jar of stem ginger at the same time. I had once heard Mrs Willet say that they were 'both very partial' to ginger.

As always, it was bliss to stay at Amy's. Her house is quiet and beautiful, and looks out upon a southern-sloping garden and the Hampshire hills in the distance. My bedroom had the same aspect, and a bowl of early pale pink hyacinths scented the room.

'How clever of you to get them in bloom by Christmas!' I said. 'Mine are only an inch high, and they were planted at the beginning of term.'

'Choose Anne-Marie,' advised Amy, 'and leave them in the dark for at least two months. Then they roar ahead once you get them into the light.'

They obviously did for Amy, I thought, but would they for me?

Bent church, where Amy and James were regular attendants, was splendidly decorated on Christmas Day with arum lilies as well as Christmas roses and the usual evergreens. There was an air of opulence about the building which our modest St Patrick's lacked at Fairacre. A rich carpet covered the chancel, and the vicar's vestments were embroidered in gold thread, so much more ornate than the simple white cassock, laundered by Mrs Willet, which clothed Gerald Partridge.

But Bent church itself had a cathedral-like splendour, with side chapels and a roof of fan-vaulting. The choir was twice the size of our own, and obviously more musically proficient. The processional hymn had a beautiful and intricate descant which soared to the equally beautiful and intricate roof above, and raised all our spirits with it. Altogether, the service was gloriously inspiring, and I said so to Amy as we walked back.

'Our vicar,' said James, 'always excels himself at the major church festivals, and puts on a good show.'

It was said quite seriously, but I was rather taken aback by the last few words. Was there something theatrical about the service? Was there a display of pomp and ceremony which would not have been in order at St Patrick's?

And what if there were? The whole service had been to the glory of God and surely, I thought, it was only right and proper for the finest music and the most splendid flowers and vestments to be used to heighten the impact of the best-loved of all church festivals.

We needed a rest after our Christmas dinner, but as soon as we could move again Amy suggested that we all went for a walk before it grew dark.

James was always at his gayest in the open air. As a young man he had been a great sportsman, and even now had the litheness and spring of a twenty-year-old. He was a handsome fellow, and I quite understood how he had appealed to Amy.

He had the knack of making any woman feel that she was the only person in the world that interested him. He had a way of gazing intently into one's face, and although I was pretty sure that it was because he was short-sighted and too vain to wear spectacles, the result was still very pleasant.

The countryside south of Caxley was more wooded than that around Fairacre, and we scuffed our shoes amongst drifts of dead leaves as we threaded our way through a

nearby copse. The bare branches creaked and rustled in a light breeze above us, and on the ground the rosettes of primrose leaves were already showing. It was heartening to see that the honeysuckle was already in tiny leaf, and blackbirds were calling to each other as if this mild weather were really spring.

We emerged from the wood into a wide meadow where sheep grazed. The grass was pale and dry, but the animals ate steadily, only raising their heads briefly to survey us as, jaws rotating methodically, they gazed at us without interest.

There was a stile before us which James vaulted in fine fashion, but Amy and I rested our arms upon it and gazed at the view. The horizon was the sort of blue one sees in Japanese prints, and beyond that, we knew, was the sea some seventy miles away. It was so peaceful and quiet that we might have been looking at a landscape by John Constable, all thought of towns, traffic and the madness of men left far behind.

'Are you coming?' called James from the distance.

Amy looked at me questioningly.

'As you like,' I said.

'We're going back,' she shouted.

James nodded and retraced his steps. He made another gallant attempt to clear the stile, but caught his foot on the top bar and fell.

He was unhurt, and lay on the ground laughing.

'You shouldn't show off at your age,' said Amy sternly.

But she was kind enough to haul him upright.

On Boxing Day Amy announced that a few old friends were coming for a midday drink.

'Everyone will be having cold turkey anyway,' she said, 'so that no one will have to worry about rushing back to see if all's well in the oven.'

'But they might have mince pies,' I pointed out.

'That's their lookout,' replied my friend, filling up delectable little silver receptacles, which my grandmother used to call 'bonbon dishes', with roasted almonds, cashew nuts and minute cheesy morsels.

'Do I know any of them?'

'John and Mary from next door. Bella and Bob from down the lane, and two very nice bachelors I wanted you to meet.'

My heart sank. Amy is an inveterate matchmaker, and after years of patient – and impatient – explanations on my part, she still harbours the hope that she will one day turn me into a middle-aged bride.

I forbore to question her more on the matter, but

carried the little dishes into the sitting room and disposed them in strategic positions, only to watch Amy positioning them elsewhere when she came in.

The guests duly arrived. The married couples I had met before, and we greeted each other affectionately. We all agreed that the weather was unseasonably mild – and quoted: 'a green Christmas makes a full churchyard' – but what a blessing there was no snow! (Who, apart from Bing Crosby, we said, wanted a white Christmas?)

Both bachelors were of a suitable age to be married to me one day should any of the three of us feel inclined, but they were cheerful company, and prattled away about ski-ing and cheese dishes.

I was not much help to the one who was going ski-ing, but his companion, who had been given nearly three pounds of cheese for Christmas, was given a few recipes from my memory.

'Would you like some?' he asked eagerly. 'I could easily run over to Fairacre with a lump of Cheddar or Stilton – no bother at all.'

'It's terribly kind of you,' I replied, 'but I've been given quite a lot of cheese too, and shall have the deuce of a time eating it up.'

Afterwards, when all our guests had gone home to their cold turkey, and possibly over-cooked mince pies, Amy chided me for turning down Osbert's kind offer.

'It would have been so nice for you to meet again,' she said, 'I'm sure he was hoping to see you in the New Year.'

'He'll probably be giving a bumper cheese and wine party,' I said.

'That's possible,' agreed Amy, looking pleased. 'Good! You're bound to be asked.'

*

I left James and Amy after lunch on Wednesday so that I could drive home in the light.

I found Mrs Pringle just about to go home after putting my house to rights.

'And you had a good Christmas?' I enquired.

'A bit of an upset early on,' said she, 'but Christmas Day and Boxing Day went well, considering.'

I did not ask about the 'bit of an upset' in case it took too long to recount, but turned to wider issues.

'And all's well in Fairacre?'

'You'll be sorry to hear that Mr Mawne has gone to hospital.'

'Oh dear! What's wrong?'

A mulish look came over Mrs Pringle's countenance. 'That,' she said, 'I am not prepared to say.'

'Not prepared to say?' I echoed, absolutely dumbfounded.

If there is one thing Mrs Pringle loves beyond all others, it is the recounting, with nauseating details, of any ailment which has cropped up. As a squeamish woman I have suffered often in this way, and the thought that Mrs Pringle was willing to pass up a golden opportunity to discomfit me was more than I could comprehend.

My undisguised surprise prompted her to continue, however. 'It's a *gentleman's* complaint,' she said austerely, 'and farther than that I will not go.'

'I quite understand,' I managed to say. I was certainly not agog to hear about Henry Mawne's afflictions, gentlemanly or otherwise, and offered to run her home to change the subject.

'Thank you, but no! I have to go to the Post Office for my pension, and Alice Willet's for a sheet she's sides-to-middling for me.'

I accompanied her to the door. There she turned, and fixed me with a glinting eye. 'As well you know, I do my best not to speak Mr Mawne's name after *all that bother*, but I thought it was only Christian to mention it.'

'Oh, all that's forgiven and forgotten ages ago,' I said easily.

'Not by me it isn't,' said she implacably, and swept out to her errands.

CHAPTER 8

Trouble for Josh Pringle

'All that bother' to which Mrs Pringle referred had happened some months before.

After Miss Parr's death, her nephew John Parr inherited her lovely house. It was turned into three flats, and he kept the ground floor one.

As he was abroad on business a great deal, and later got married and moved away, Fairacre did not see much of John Parr but he had let the first floor flat to an acquaintance of his, a retired schoolmaster called Henry Mawne.

The village took to Henry Mawne. He was a friendly soul, and the vicar soon became grateful to him for his ease with figures and his willingness to straighten out some church accounts which had become sadly entangled by our highly literate, but completely innumerate, vicar.

He was a great bird-lover and had written several books on ornithology. He contributed to *The Caxley Chronicle* on topical nature matters, and altogether was considered a most welcome inhabitant of Fairacre.

He lived alone, and of course the usual rumours flew around:

(1) He was a widower, and his wife had died of cancer,

(2) He was a widower, and his wife had been killed in (a) a car crash (b) a train crash (c) a plane crash,

(3) He was a bachelor and had looked after his aged mother until matrimony seemed out of the question,

(4) He had been married but his wife had left him, and he was now (a) divorced (b) in a state of secret and well-hidden grief.

It was not long before the village made up its corporate mind that Henry Mawne and I should make a match of it. It was some time before this embarrassing fact percolated my innocent head and was then very difficult to ignore.

Mrs Pringle made arch remarks. Even Gerald Partridge meandered on about the happy outcome of marriages made 'when the partners are of mature years' and I began to get quite alarmed.

To give Henry Mawne his due, he seemed to be unaware of the gossip flying about, and apart from accompanying me to a concert in Caxley and bringing me a rather untidy bunch of daffodils picked from the thousands in his garden in the spring, he did not pay me any particularly ardent attentions.

But one day Mrs Pringle had gone too far. After telling me how much 'poor Mr Mawne' could do with a woman about the place, she told me that 'he was fair eating his heart out – and the whole village knew it.'

That did it. I told her that to repeat idle gossip could not only be hurtful but scandalous, and that I should have to consider consulting my solicitor.

At this, Mrs Pringle retaliated by giving in her notice – much to my secret relief.

She was away for a little over a week on this occasion, and very pleasant it was without her morose presence. Her niece Minnie, as mad as a March hare, came 'to oblige' in the school, but it was obvious that she could never be allowed to take on permanent duties.

In the end, of course, my old sparring partner returned, but I had been so fierce with her that she did her best never to mention Henry Mawne's name again in my presence.

In fact, Henry's wife turned up some time later, much to my relief and the disappointment of Fairacre in general. They had had their differences, and evidently had lived apart for some two years, but had decided to throw in their lot together again. It appeared to work, and I grew very fond of vociferous Mrs Mawne as the years passed.

But at that time, I was the unwilling recipient of a great deal of sympathy from neighbours who thought I might be heartbroken.

Mrs Pringle's silent tribute to my feelings expressed itself in a fine plump partridge, ready for roasting. I accepted it partly as an expression of condolence, but also as a peace-offering, and very good it was when it was dished up.

'The bit of an upset' which had preceded Mrs Pringle's Christmas that year, was recounted to me by Mr Willet. It involved the black sheep of the Pringle family, Josh Pringle from Springbourne.

It seems that as Christmas approached, his numerous children began to clamour for such things as a Christmas tree, a turkey, and, above all, presents.

Josh shook off these scandalous demands until his wife, unusually outspoken, added her weight to the children's.

'Of course you must get 'em something,' she told Josh when the children were in bed. 'Pity you never paid into a club like most people do, then we could have a few sweets and oranges and that to put in their stockings.'

'They gets all they need,' replied Josh. 'Anyway, clubs is your business. You gets the housekeeping.'

His wife gave a sarcastic laugh. 'That'll be the day! You give me what's in your pocket now and I'll see what I can do.'

'There ain't nothing in my pocket.'

'Gone on beer, I suppose. Self, self, self, and them poor kids without a present between them.'

Josh swore, rose from his armchair and walked out into the night to get a bit of peace.

As he mooched along the dark lanes, he pondered about Christmas and its expense. He supposed he would have to provide the minimum for the festivities or he would never hear the last of it. The thing was, where to get the money?

He had been given two weeks' work on a building site and the wages had gone already. Not only on beer, but also on one of those 'dead certs' in the three-thirty at Newbury which had unseated its rider in the first fifty yards, and run happily unencumbered, with its fellow racers, finishing well down the field.

Turning over the uncertainties of life in general, Josh plodded along the miry lane until he found himself on the outskirts of Fairacre. It was then that he remembered his brother Fred. Could he possibly touch him for a quid or two? He knew better than to approach Maud Pringle – she wouldn't give anyone a brass farthing, and a clump on the ear may well be collected by an importuning relative, Christmas or no Christmas. It had happened to Josh before, and he was not going to ask for another.

By this time he had reached Fred Pringle's house. He walked silently to the back door, his feet making no noise. Josh was not a poacher for nothing, and had deceived many a gamekeeper with his noiseless movements.

He could see Maud at her ironing through the kitchen window. She was late at her task, although Josh was not to know that, for Minnie had not returned from the hospital on the bus expected. She had arrived with the patient, happily freed from peas in his ears, two hours later than intended, and by that time Mrs Pringle had had more than enough of Josh's family. Some paper chains made the room gay, and a large red paper bell hung close above his sister-in-law's head.

There was no sign of Fred, but he might well be in the sitting room watching telly. Having come this far, Josh decided to knock and trust his luck. He would certainly stay well back out of arm's length of Fred's wife. He doubted if the Christmas spirit of peace on earth and goodwill to all men would extend to embrace him in Maud's eyes.

When the door opened Mrs Pringle gave a gasp. 'And what do *you* want?'

'Just passing. Thought I'd wish you a merry Christmas.'

Mrs Pringle snorted. 'You'd better see Fred. He's down the shed. I'm busy.'

With that the door slammed. It was no more than Josh had expected, and at least he had not been injured. He made his way down the concrete path, beneath the clothes line, to Fred's shed at the bottom of the garden, hard by the chicken run.

There was a queer droning noise coming from behind the broken door. Josh listened for a moment, decided it was only his brother humming and knocked.

The droning stopped abruptly.

'What's up?' Fred sounded startled. Josh opened the door.

'Good lord! What brings you here?' said Fred.

'Just thought I'd wish you a merry Christmas,' replied

Josh, 'happened to be passing like.'

'My Maud seen you?'

'She spoke to me at the back door.'

'I wonder you didn't get a clip round the ear.'

'What you up to?' said Josh, feeling it was wise to change the subject.

A pile of matchsticks, some stout cardboard and a pot of evil-smelling glue lay on the bench before his brother. He was sitting on a backless kitchen chair which looked vaguely familiar. It must have come from their old home, he decided. Funny that Fred should have kept it, and funnier still that Maud had not thrown it out.

'Calendars!' replied Fred. 'See, I makes one of them little wooden houses – *chalets*, they call 'em. It stands out in relief like and I hangs a calendar underneath. Go like hot cakes down "The Beetle and Wedge" for three bob a time.

Not that I dares go in there with our Maud, but the landlord sends the money down.'

The mention of 'The Beetle and Wedge' combined with money acted as a spur to Josh's intentions.

'Very nice,' he said ingratiatingly, 'specially at Christmas. Could do with a bit of cash myself to tell the truth.'

'Oh ah!'

'The kids, you know. Need a few things, and I'm fair strapped for money. Times have been hard lately.'

'Thought you had work at Bailey's yard.'

'Ah! All that went on bills that come in.'

There was silence while Fred stuck on another matchstick.

'So you've come here for a loan, have you?'

'Well, if you could see your way clear, Fred, I'd be much obliged. I've got some beating coming up after Christmas. Three big shoots – ought to make me a bit. I could pay you back early in the New Year.'

Again silence fell. A hen squawked nearby. A large vehicle rumbled in the village street.

'That's the last Caxley,' observed Fred, picking up another matchstick. 'Must be half past seven.'

Josh was content to wait. He knew old Fred. Everything took time to decide.

'I see you've got one of our Mum's old chairs,' he remarked.

'Ah! Just the right height for this job. Maud was all for chucking it out, but I brought it down here.'

'We had good times as kids,' said Josh. There was a sentimental whine in his tone, and Fred was not deceived. Best get rid of him he supposed, stirring the glue pot, before he started crying over old times. At this rate he'd never get the roof done, let alone the doorway.

'I've got mighty little myself,' said Fred, dismissing the old memories bit, 'but you can have two quid.'

He rummaged in a back pocket and handed over two crumpled pound notes.

'You're a good sort, Fred. I won't forget.'

'You'd better not! It's a loan, not a Christmas present. You see you pay me back after your beating.'

'I'll do that, Fred. That I will. That's a promise.'

He held out a dirty hand. Reluctantly Fred shook it.

'Now I've been and dropped that matchstick, blast it!' he said.

'Best not let Maud hear you a-swearing,' laughed Josh and made his way into the night.

When Fred Pringle finally emerged from his haven, leaving two calendars to dry on the bench, his wife was waiting for him in the living room.

'And what did that waster want?'

'Old Josh? Oh, he just dropped in, you know. Christmas, and all that.'

Fred's airy tone did not deceive Maud.

'I asked what he *wanted*,' persisted the lady. 'Did you give him money?'

Fred had a sudden coughing attack.

'You'd best have your cocoa now,' said Mrs Pringle, 'we'll talk then.'

She departed into the kitchen and soon returned with two steaming mugs on a tray, and the usual pair of digestive biscuits which constituted their bed-time snack.

'Now, let's have the truth, Fred Pringle,' she said flatly. 'How much, and why?'

'Two quid, and because he's my brother,' replied Fred, who thought he might as well get the whole business over and done with.

'You're a bigger fool than I thought,' was his wife's

comment, stirring two spoonfuls of sugar into Fred's mug. 'You'll never see that again!'

'He knows it's only a loan. He's got money due from beating after Christmas.'

'If I was a betting woman,' said Mrs Pringle, 'which I am glad to say I'm not, I would bet my last penny that Josh Pringle will never pay you back. You're a fool, Fred, and weak with it. You should have sent him packing.'

'At Christmas time?'

'Particularly at Christmas time,' said Mrs Pringle, 'that's when he needs it most. If I know that good-for-nothing brother of yours he's already in "The Beetle and Wedge" drinking his way through your cash.'

'I was thinking of his poor kids.'

'His *poor kids*,' replied Maud, who had seen more than enough of them that day, 'are Josh's affair, not yours. Let him provide for his own.'

And with that she banged the two empty mugs on the tray, and swept out into the kitchen.

She was right of course.

Josh Pringle had gone to the pub in Fairacre's High Street, and there quaffed three pints of beer before closing time. He was not drunk when he emerged from the pub, but the path was slippery. He crashed to the ground outside Mr Willet's gate, letting out a great bellow.

Bob Willet, busy shutting up his hen house, heard the cry and went to investigate and, seeing who it was, assumed that Josh was drunk.

'Here, give us your hand,' he said, 'and remember to take more water with it.'

Josh staggered to his feet, gave a yelp of pain, and flung his arms round Mr Willet for support.

'It's me ankle,' gasped Josh, 'bin and done it in.'

He was certainly in pain and, although he smelt of beer, Mr Willet was pretty sure he was not completely intoxicated.

'You'd best come in a minute, and let Alice have a look.'

Leaning heavily on the shorter man, Josh hobbled up the path.

Alice Willet, who was getting ready for bed and had already taken down her bun and transformed it into a wispy grey plait, was not pleased to see their guest.

'Josh has done somethin' to his ankle,' explained Bob, depositing the patient in an armchair with a sigh of relief.

'Better let me see,' said Alice resignedly.

The state of Josh's socks gave her far more of a shock than his injuries. The former were tattered and decidedly noisome. His ankle was already beginning to swell.

'It's only a sprain,' said Alice. 'I'll tie a wet bandage round it.'

She departed into the kitchen and Bob Willet decided to open a window. When his wife returned, the air was much fresher.

'See if you can stand on it,' said Alice, 'before I strap you up.'

Josh heaved himself upright, gave a yell and collapsed back into the chair.

'I reckon I've bin and broke it,' he despaired. 'And I've got beating to do next week.'

'You'll be all right by then,' said Bob. 'Just have to keep it up over the next couple of days.'

Alice knelt down and began to swathe the ankle with a long strip of clean linen which had once been part of one of Bob's shirts.

'Gawd!' yelped the patient. On seeing Alice's scandalised face, he apologised.

'You'll have to put up with a bit of pain,' said his nurse.

'But how am I going to get home?'

Bob and Alice exchanged glances. Getting him home was the ardent desire of both, but it was now ten-thirty, and who would be going to Springbourne at that time?

Inspiration came to Mr Willet as his wife secured the last two inches of the wet bandage.

'What about Chalky White? I believe he's on night shift at the signal box this week. I'll nip round and see. Won't be a tick.'

He vanished through the door leaving Josh and Alice surveying each other.

'I'm real sorry about this,' began Josh. 'Your old man thought I was drunk, I believe.'

'Well, it wouldn't be the first time,' commented Alice

tartly. She was longing for her bed, but her natural kindness triumphed, and she asked if Josh would like a cup of tea. Good for shock, she said.

'No thanks, duck. You done enough.'

They sank into silence.

Meanwhile, some hundred yards away, Bob Willet was explaining his problem to Chalky, who owned a battered Ford of uncertain age because his hours of work as a signalman were erratic.

'It would be Josh, wouldn't it?' he groaned. 'Fair reeking of ale, no doubt. And a good half mile out of my way. How's the time?'

He looked at the clock on the mantelpiece, then hauled out a silver pocket watch from his uniform waistcoat pocket. He looked carefully from one to the other, while Bob secretly fumed. Chalky always took his time.

'Well, it's like this,' said Chalky at last, 'I have to be at Fox Bottom at midnight to relieve young Skinner. Now I reckons to get there at *five to* at the outside – *ten to* would be better – and I've got to have a bite before I go while Mother cuts me sandwiches. D'you follow?'

Bob said that yes, yes, he followed.

'So if you can get him here before, let's say, eleven-fifteen pip emma, I'll deliver him to Springbourne.'

Bob broke into a torrent of thanks, but Chalky White raised a hand for silence.

'I'm not doing it *willingly*, I don't mind admitting, but to oblige you and Alice.'

'Very grateful we are too, Chalky,' Bob assured him, and hurried back with the good news.

Their visitor seemed quite lively, but his poor Alice,

thought Bob, looked ready to drop. He went into action at once.

'Chalky'll drop you home, Josh. We'll take it easy. One arm round my shoulders, and my old blackthorn stick in the other hand. Let's try it.'

In this fashion, Josh limped to the door, then turned to Alice. 'Thanks for the help. I'm real grateful, Mrs Willet.' He held up the stick. 'See you when I return this.'

'No need to return it,' said Bob, urging him through the door. 'Keep it as a Christmas present. I've got half a dozen walkin' sticks. Now, watch the step, and put your weight on me.'

Alice watched them out of sight, put up the fireguard and went thankfully upstairs to bed.

Half an hour later, Bob Willet fell into bed beside her.

'What an evenin'! Thank heavens we got him to old Chalky's. I'll take a few eggs round to them tomorrow to thank him for helpin' us out.'

'That Josh!' murmured Alice. 'The yarns he tells! He'd been to see Fred, he said, and Fred had given him two pounds.'

'Bet that didn't go farther than "The Beetle",' observed Bob, with a mighty yawn.

'I don't think you should've given him that stick, you know, Bob. You was always fond of it.'

'I'd never see it again, anyway,' said her husband. 'No point in *lendin'* anything to our Josh. You'd never get it back.'

'Well, he said Fred Pringle *lent* him the two pounds.'

'Fred Pringle,' said Mr Willet, 'is a fool, and always was. Well, look who he married!'

CHAPTER 9

Spinsters, 'Splashem' and Spring

Although Mrs Pringle did her best to distance herself from what she termed 'that Springbourne lot', Minnie Pringle turned up far more frequently than her aunt-by-marriage wished.

In the fullness of time, the third child born out of wedlock arrived, and not long afterwards Mrs Pringle told me some surprising news.

'Believe it or not, Miss Read, but that Minnie is getting married.'

'Good heavens! It hardly seems worth the bother, does it?'

I was squatting down by the map cupboard, trying to extricate a large piece of cardboard which I needed for mounting the children's pictures.

The map cupboard is a dangerous place to work in: furled maps, ranging from 'Great Britain's Possessions Overseas' (somewhat out of date) to 'The Disposition of the Tribes of Israel' (equally out of date) not to mention 'Aids to Resuscitation in case of Inhalation of Gas' (fat chance in Fairacre where we have no gas) to 'The Muscular System of the Human Body'.

As well as these aids to education, all the awkward objects which have no real home seem to find their way into this cupboard: odd shoes, a broken croquet mallet, a moth-eaten rug, an archaic oil lamp and a cardboard box containing a jumble of jigsaw pieces which have lost their way over the years and share the space with an assortment of stray building bricks, bone counters, odd dominoes and the like.

'That cupboard,' remarked Mrs, Pringle, 'is a menace. That great Union Jack fell out on me Monday afternoon, and brought up a lump the size of a pigeon's egg.'

She put a hand to her head dramatically, while I tugged out the cardboard sheet successfully, wondering meanwhile why it is always a *pigeon's* egg. Why not a bantam's, or an owl's or even an everyday hen's egg?

'So who's the lucky man?' I asked, dusting myself down. It seemed rather silly to get married when Minnie had been doing as nicely as she was capable of, without benefit of the clergy, all this time.

'Quite a nice steady chap,' said Mrs Pringle. 'A widower with five children, called Ern.'

I began to see the reason for this marriage.

'But will Minnie be able to cope with such a large family? That will make eight altogether, won't it?'

'Well, one or two are off his hands now, married or working in Caxley, so there will only be a few home to sleep, and the biggest girl's quite helpful. And you see, he's got a council house, so Minnie will be getting a place of her own at last.'

It sounded as though it would be uncomfortably crowded, but Mrs Pringle seemed to think the whole affair was a good arrangement.

'Minnie wanted a white wedding,' she went on, 'with some of the small children as bridesmaids and pages and

109

that. She was all for bells and the organ as well, but her mum pointed out it would cost a pretty penny.'

'I should have thought a quiet wedding at Caxley Registry Office would have suited the occasion.'

'That's just it! It *is* an occasion! After all, every girl likes to remember her wedding day. I can quite see why Minnie wanted it all nice and lovely.'

I did not feel that this was the right time to remind Mrs Pringle that a bride in white was meant to represent virginity, and that Minnie could hardly be included in that state with three young children in attendance.

'So what with one thing or another, our Minnie's got a blue dress with a matching coat, and making do with a white hat she got at the Plymouth Brethren jumble last month.'

'Sounds splendid.'

'And I'm lending her my white confirmation Bible to carry.'

I privately hoped she would hold it the right way up. Minnie cannot read, but probably there would be no need to refer to it during the ceremony so the Bible would be for effect only.

'That's the *borrowed*,' said Mrs Pringle.

'The borrowed what?' I asked bewildered.

Mrs Pringle tut-tutted crossly.

'Something old,
Something new,
Something borrowed
And something blue', she quoted. 'Well, my Bible's the *borrowed*, see?'

At this moment, Joe Coggs rushed in to say that Ernest had got himself locked in the lavatory, and was hollering something awful.

Minnie's nuptials were forgotten as I went to investigate.

I did not come across Mrs Pringle during the rest of the day so heard no more of Minnie's plans for some time.

But that evening Amy called on her way back from Oxford, and while we were drinking coffee and admiring her purchases, the subject of matrimony cropped up. It often does with Amy.

'This is such a dear little house,' she said, 'such a shame that it only has you living in it.'

'It doesn't complain,' I retorted, 'and neither do I.'

'You know, the older you get,' continued Amy, changing tactics slightly, 'the more difficult it is going to be to find somebody suitable.'

'Don't worry about it. I honestly prefer to be single.'

'Of course you feel that way now. But what about the time when you retire? You're bound to be lonely.'

'Don't you believe it! I shall kick up my heels and nip off to foreign parts, squandering my hard-earned pension in all directions.'

'But again, it would be so much more fun if you had a companion.'

'Why? They might want to do the things I don't want to do. Now I can please myself.'

'That's a very *selfish* point of view,' said Amy severely. 'Anyway, it's not just holidays I'm thinking of. It's the general day-to-day companionship you need. Besides,' she added, catching sight of an untidy pile of books by the sofa, 'it might make you tidier, if you had someone else to consider.'

'Mrs Pringle comes tomorrow,' I comforted her. 'I shall be thoroughly "bottomed", and not be able to find anything.'

111

'Haven't you ever met anyone who attracts you? You were quite pretty when we were at college.'

'Thanks for the compliment. And yes, of course I've seen lots of men who are attractive. Your James, for one, but you snapped him up first.'

Amy looked smug. 'Yes, I did, didn't I? And I don't regret it.' She began to look pensive and then added: 'Really,' rather doubtfully.

To cheer her up I told her about Minnie's wedding.

'I'm glad to hear she's been persuaded from wearing white,' she said. 'What are you giving her for a wedding present?'

'I didn't propose to give her anything. Mrs Pringle is giving her a set of saucepans and her old mincer, if she can find the wing nut that holds all the blades together.'

'Is Minnie capable of managing a mincer?'

'I shouldn't think so for a minute, and if she does get it to work, I'm sure it will be Minnie's fingers that will go first through the contraption.'

'What coffee is this?' asked Amy, swilling the dregs of her cup round and round.

'This Week's Offer from the shop in the village.'

'As I thought,' said Amy, and drank no more.

After Amy had gone I pottered about my domestic duties. There was a blouse to iron, some clothes to wash, the window box to water and Tibby's belated supper to put down for that fastidious animal.

Rain had set in, and I went about my affairs to the accompaniment of raindrops pattering against the window, and a musical trickling of water into the butt outside the kitchen door.

It was all very peaceful. I relish my time alone in the

school house, dealing rather inefficiently with my chores. This evening I pondered on Amy's urgings towards matrimony.

I am, far too often for my liking, the object of my friends' solicitude. Why this overwhelming desire to see everyone married? Quite a few of us, both men and women, are perfectly satisfied with the single state and seem to lead useful and happy lives.

At this point, doubts assailed me. Was this being too smug and selfish? Certainly we did not have to consider other people in the home – husbands, children and so on. So were we really leading useful lives?

Well, I jolly well am, I told myself robustly. I run my school with fair success. I do my best to help in the village, handing over clothes to the jumble sale (which I almost always regret later, as I could have done with them myself), I occasionally stand in for the organist, I do my stint of washing up at the Women's Institute, and a bit of sitting-in for friends with young children. I help at local fêtes and concerts, stick up posters, deliver leaflets for worthy causes, and lend an ear to those who come to me for advice, and give them coffee as well.

At this point, my mind veered to This Week's Offer. Was it really as dreadful as Amy seemed to think? It had tasted all right to me, but then I did not have Amy's rarefied palate.

Perhaps Amy was right – not just about the coffee, but the selfish and narrow life I lead. But what could I do? I was in no position to put the world to rights. There was no way in which I could feed the Third World, stop global warfare, cope with sea, air and land pollution and other immense problems, except for adding my signature to the appropriate forms.

No, I decided, it was just a case of soldiering on from day to day in one's own little sphere.

'You in your small corner, and I in mine,' I sang to Tibby. The cat, startled, shot out of the window.

Of course, it was nice of Amy, I thought charitably, to be so concerned about my solitary state, but also decidedly irritating. She *would* dredge up those middle-aged men! As bad as Mrs Pringle and the others in Fairacre, who had made my life uncomfortable over Henry Mawne.

I began to put out the breakfast things on the kitchen table, ready for the morning, still pondering on the mentality of those who are intent on pressing matrimony upon those who don't need it. Had Minnie's approaching nuptials really set off a whole evening's train of thought?

The clock struck ten, and I pulled myself together. Hot milk, and bed with a book. What bliss! Why, if I had a husband he might want the light off, or dislike me sipping hot milk! He would probably snore too.

Feeling delightfully smug I surveyed the kitchen table. I saw that I had picked up Tibby's plate, still decorated with the remains of Pussi-luv, and set it carefully at my breakfast place.

'That's what comes of thinking,' I said aloud, and went to bed.

The wet weather continued for weeks. Mrs Pringle grew more and more morose as wet footmarks sullied the floors, and raincoats dripped from their pegs.

Most days we were unable to let the children play outside. The consequence was that they grew peevish with being cooped up all day. The dog-eared comics grew even shabbier, the 'playtime toys' grubbier, and the children longed to rush about in the fresh air as keenly as I wanted them to do so.

Occasionally, when the rain stopped at the appropriate time, I let them out, with terrible threats about what would happen to them if they played 'Splashem'.

This game, which cannot be Fairacre's alone, is simplicity itself. All it needs is some puddles and plenty of unsuspecting victims.

The idea is to wait until a child strays near a puddle and then to jump heavily into the water, sending a cascade over the victim. The harder you jump, the higher the spray, and it has been known to drench a small child from the neck down. Wild cries of 'Splashem' accompany this simple pursuit, and roars of laughter. It is a game which I forbid in the playground, with some success, but what happens on the way home I shudder to think, despite my exhortations.

Mrs Pringle, of course, is as equally opposed to 'Splashem' as I am, but with her floors rather than the unhappy victims in mind.

'I see that Jimmy Waites and Joe Coggs jumping about in that long puddle by the Post Office. Their shoes was fair sopped. It's time the Council done something about that puddle. What do we pay rates for, I'd like to know?'

'I hope you ticked them off.'

'I done my best, but kids these days gets away with murder.'

She bent down to scrape something sticky from the classroom floor with her finger nail.

'Blessed bubble gum!' she grumbled. 'Our Minnie used to give it to hers until I told her I wouldn't have the stuff in my house.'

'I meant to ask you, how did the wedding go?'

She straightened up, wheezing heavily, and seated herself on the front desk. To my surprise, a maudlin smile spread over her face.

115

'Oh, it was a real lovely wedding! Minnie looked a treat in blue, and she had his youngest girl as bridesmaid. It wouldn't have looked too good to have had her own children.'

'Quite,' I said.

'I left the baby in the pram just outside the church porch, and looked after the other two in the back pew. They wasn't too bad, considering. His four was further up the church. Not very well turned out, I thought, and no hats.'

'People don't seem to bother about hats these days.'

'Well, I certainly do. I bought a real beauty in Caxley. Navy blue straw with a white feather ornament. Very smart. I always think navy and white looks *classy*, and it don't date.'

'Did you have a wedding breakfast?'

'We did indeed! In Springbourne village hall, and though the toilet arrangements there are not what they should be, we had some lovely ham and salad.'

'So now Minnie is really settling down,' I said, one eye on the clock, and hoping to see my school cleaner depart.

'Well, she's *married*,' she said cautiously, 'but *settled* I'd not like to say. You can never tell with Minnie.'

And with this ominous comment she made her way into the lobby to see that the doormat was thoroughly used by the children.

Much to the relief of everyone in Fairacre, the wet spell of weather was followed by days of sunshine.

Blankets and quilts, coats and curtains blew on the clothes lines. Mats and rugs were draped over hedges ready for thorough beating, as the long delayed spring cleaning got on its way.

Mrs Pringle caught the fever and insisted on tackling my house room by room. I took to staying a little longer in school to miss the severe censure I faced about my house-keeping methods.

She started on the bedrooms and I was unfortunate enough to encounter her on the first occasion.

'I've been droring my finger along the top of this pelmet,' she told me, from her vantage post on a bedroom chair, 'and you could write your name in the dust, that you could. When Mrs Hope was here, she had a feather broom in *constant use*! Tops of doors, picture rails, curtain tops, she done 'em all regular. Everything smelt as sweet as a nut.'

'It doesn't *smell*,' I protested.

'You gets used to it,' she retorted. 'Living in your own mess, you gets used to it. Like pigs,' she added malevolently.

I was about to retire worsted in this battle, but Mrs Pringle called me back.

'I'll take these curtains home with me and give the poor things a bit of soap and water. So you'd better let me have your summer ones to put up while I'm here.'

'I don't have any summer ones,' I told her, 'those are simply *The Curtains*. They stay up all the year round.'

Mrs Pringle gasped, and nearly fell off the chair with shock.

'You mean to say you've no spares in the linen cupboard?'

'That's right.' I was beginning to enjoy myself.

'The gentry,' said Mrs Pringle, 'always has two sets, winter and summer.'

'I'm not gentry.'

'That's *quite* plain,' she said offensively, 'but even poor

117

Mrs Hope had velvet for winter and sprigged cotton for summer. Made them herself too,' she added for good measure, 'and her a chronic invalid.'

When Mrs Hope's name is invoked I know that I don't stand a chance. My predecessor in the school house must have been a perfect housewife.

'Well, take them by all means,' I said, 'they are probably ready for a wash.'

'That's more than true,' she panted, beginning to struggle with the hooks, 'but what about bed time, when you're undressing?'

'No one will be watching,' I assured her, 'only the birds in the garden, and they'll be roosting by the time I go to bed.'

'My old mother,' she said, 'would have been scandalised at having no curtains to the bedroom windows.'

Mrs Pringle's mother has been dead for many years, so I forbore to comment on her possible disapproval and made for the door.

'Mrs Hope —' began Mrs Pringle.

But by that time I was well out of earshot.

School, in this balmy spell of weather, returned to normal and 'Splashem' was a thing of the past.

We had rather more nature walks than the timetable allowed, and thoroughly enjoyed finding spring flowers for the nature table. Celandines and primroses starred the banks and coppices, and white and blue violets hid themselves in the dry grass under Mr Roberts' hedgerows.

Birds were already nesting, and some still building, flying across our path trailing long grasses or struggling with beaks full of moss or feathers. Soon the swallows would be back, searching in cottage porches and barns for the nests they left behind the autumn before.

It was a time of great hope. There were lambs in the fields, the sun was warm, and the hedges were showing a tender green.

Our little procession was in high spirits, and people waved to us from their gardens or windows, deserting their hoeing or dusting for a few minutes to watch us on our way to the windy downs.

It is at times like this that I relish my life as a teacher in a country school. For me, there is nothing so satisfying as life in a village. It is good to know everybody, and good to be known. Occasionally, I resent the interest in my affairs, as in the case of Henry Mawne's attentions, but it is far better, I tell myself, to know that I am of interest rather than to be ignored.

And then the job itself is so varied. How many people

119

could walk away from their desks, their papers, their telephones, and take a refreshing stroll among grass and trees, with rooks cawing overhead?

I thought of the glimpses one gets from the train, running into London, showing vast open-plan offices with row upon row of desks, strong overhead lighting and a regiment of workers, as confined as battery hens. No doubt these soulless places had windows hermetically sealed, and a system of air-conditioning liable to give the unfortunate inmates sinus trouble, sore throats and headaches. How much better to have one's shoes clogged with the pale chalky mud of the downs – despite the wrath of Mrs Pringle. At least our lungs were filled with exhilarating fresh air, and we were bursting with energy.

There was something terrifying too about the vast numbers of people glimpsed in those offices and factories. The pressure on space, seen possibly at its worst on the platforms of stations at rush hour, was incredibly depressing and frightening. Here at Fairacre, our little school numbered less than thirty children, and it looked as if those numbers would fall again before long, a fact which brought its own problems, but fortunately not that of over-crowding and its attendant ills.

By this time, the nature walk had left the village, and had taken a steep muddy track uphill. On our right a flock of Mr Roberts' sheep grazed on the close-bitten grass. Above us the skylarks vied with each other, pouring down their lively trickle of song, as they pushed higher and higher towards the blue sky.

We sat down on a bank to get our breath. Most of the children were content, as I was, to sit in silence, studying the village spread out below us like a pictorial map.

The spire of St Patrick's was the salient feature, and even at this distance we could catch the gleam of the weathercock on its tip, pointing to the south-west.

Hard by the church stood our school, its playground now empty, as the infants were still in their classroom while we played truant. The vicarage and John Parr's house were hidden by the trees in their gardens, but the cottages lining the village street were visible, their thatched or weatherbeaten tiled roofs blending into the greys and browns of gardens and fields.

Beyond the church we could see Mr Roberts' herd of black and white Friesians in one field, and in the next his bay hunter cropping as industriously as the cattle. They might have been farmhouse toys at this distance, I thought. It only needed a farmer in a smock, and a milkmaid carrying a stool and pail to take one back a century.

A glance at my watch brought me to my feet.

'Nearly dinner time,' I shouted to the few stragglers in the distance, and reluctantly we gathered for our return.

I took another look at the view spread before us as we waited for the last two or three to join us. How idyllic it looked, that village of Fairacre! A stranger, gazing at it as we had done, would be forgiven for imagining that all was peace and plenty in that little community. Those of us who lived there knew better.

Arthur Coggs's house held fear and poverty for his wife and children. At the Post Office, Mr Lamb's old mother was dying, slowly and painfully, from cancer. Next door there were money troubles, and the wife was threatening to leave home. It was not all rapture in Fairacre, any more than it was elsewhere.

But at least we had space, we had wide views, we had almost unpolluted air and water and most of us had the inestimable blessing of robust health.

We began to slither down the slope, each clutching the treasures so recently collected. As well as little bunches of spring flowers, Jimmy had found three empty snail shells, large and bleached white by the weather, and I told the children that I had heard that the Romans used to collect them and eat the contents when they lived in these parts.

Eileen Burton had a rook's feather stuck behind her ear. Linda Moffat had found some late catkins and the front of her coat was yellow with pollen.

But Joseph Coggs had the most prized possession: an old nest damp from the recent rains, but still a miracle of bird-building and lined snugly with moss, feathers and shreds of wool from Mr Roberts' sheep.

He held it close to his shabby coat and his eyes were shining as he looked up at me.

'I'm going to find some little stones to put in it, like eggs,' he said.

'A good idea,' I told him, hoping he would have the

sense to keep his treasure out of his father's sight. Joe had lost things like that before.

Ernest, at the head of our procession, set up a yell.

'Dinner van's just gone up street, Miss!'

Spurred into action, we fairly sprinted up the road. First things first, we told ourselves, as we puffed dinnerward.

CHAPTER 10

Mrs Pringle Goes to Hospital

Over the years, I grew quite astute at gauging Mrs Pringle's state of mind by the barometer of her bad leg. Dragging the afflicted limb with many a sigh, heavy limping and the occasional yelp of pain on moving, all betokened umbrage on Mrs Pringle's part. I really did not think there was anything much the matter physically, but when she told me that she had to visit Caxley Cottage Hospital for some tests, I presumed that it must be something to do with her leg. Not that she said as much. I tended to hurry away with some excuse or other as I could not face the gruesome details of real or imagined symptoms.

So I only had myself to blame for my ignorance when she informed me that she had to have two or three days in hospital, or 'up the Cottage', as it is affectionately known in these parts. (We locals often have to catch 'the Caxley' to attend 'up the Cottage'.)

'Got to be there Wednesday evening, and they do me Thursday.'

'I suppose they are going to try some physiotherapy,' I said, 'or traction, or something like that.'

124

'*Traction!*' boomed Mrs Pringle. 'What, with my complaint?'

'They do use traction on legs, I believe.'

'And who said anything about legs?' she demanded.

I began to falter. Mrs Pringle's beetling brows and flashing eyes would intimidate the bravest person.

'Well, I just thought –' I began.

'*You just thought,*' echoed the lady witheringly. 'I've told you time and again I've been having Inner Trouble.'

'I'm sorry. I quite thought it was your leg giving trouble.'

'My leg,' she said, 'is always giving me trouble, but I have learnt to live with it.'

She began to limp about the classroom flicking a duster over cupboards and desks, while her last remark reminded me of a poignant little rhyme dealing with old age, which I had heard recently. It went something like this:

'I can manage my bifocals,
To my dentures I'm resigned,
I can cope with my arthritis,
But how I miss my mind!'

Whether Mrs Pringle wanted to enlighten me about the true nature of her illness I was never to know, for the children came in at that moment, and she simply called out:

'I'll let you know times and that when I comes up midday,' and departed.

The whole incident had slipped from my mind during the morning's multifarious activities, but Mrs Pringle buttonholed me in the lobby as she washed up after school dinner.

'I'll be up to do this next Wednesday, as usual. Don't have to be there till six, and Mr Partridge is giving me a lift in as the Caxley's no good that time of day. He's got to go to some Economical Council meeting, he says, so it's no bother. A real gentleman, isn't he?'

'Indeed he is.'

'But you'll have to do without me here for the rest of the week. One thing, the stoves don't need doing. With any luck, I'll be all right by the Monday, but I expect they'll say "No heavy work", like lifting desks and that, after Inner Trouble.'

'Naturally. And don't come back too soon,' I said, trying to sound solicitous rather than pleased.

'I knows my duty,' said Mrs Pringle, 'and *all being well* I should be fit for light work by then. It all depends on what they find, and if the scar is a long one.'

And on this ominous note she dropped the subject.

*

I met Mrs Partridge that evening as I walked to post an urgent letter, and she enlightened me a little more, but not much.

'How will you manage without Mrs Pringle?' she began.

'It's only for a few days, she tells me. We shall be all right.'

'Yes. As far as I can gather, it's only one of these little routine women's affairs. Quite straightforward.'

The phrase 'routine women's affairs' reminded me of Henry Mawne's 'gentleman's complaint', but naturally I forbore to comment.

In any case, I did not propose to enquire further. Mrs Partridge has had some nursing experience, and is apt to enlarge on symptoms and their treatment in unpleasantly explicit detail, and if Mrs Pringle's trouble were *'inner'*, then it would involve a conglomeration of tubes, I imagined, which would knock me cold at once.

'How's your garden?' I asked.

'Full of blossom,' she said. 'Come back with me and have a look.'

But I excused myself saying that I had books to mark and some ironing to do. This was perfectly true, but I was pretty certain that both activities would be shelved while I did that day's crossword.

A day or two later I fetched Miss Clare from Beech Green to spend the evening with me.

A few hours of Dolly Clare's company is a real refreshment of spirits. Always calm, wise and dignified, old age seems to have increased these attributes, and her memories of Fairacre School are always fascinating.

'We used to drink a lot of cocoa when I taught here before the war. Only in the winter, of course, but the

127

children enjoyed it. Somehow, cocoa seems to have gone out of fashion.'

'School milk took over, I expect,' I said. 'And some avant-garde mothers are already saying it's too fattening.'

'There weren't many over-weight children when I started teaching,' responded Dolly. 'In fact, just the other way. The farm labourers' children were definitely under-nourished, on the whole. Plenty of garden produce, of course, but mighty little meat. And somehow fish was never much relished in these parts, and so often the eggs were sold to bring in a few pence. "Us has the cracked 'uns" the children used to say.'

'Well, I'm just about to crack some for our omelettes,' I told her. 'Cheese, tomato or both, for a filling?'

She pondered for a moment and then gave me her slow sweet smile.

'Both, please. And I hear that Mrs Pringle is going to be away for a few days. Will you be able to cope?'

'Very happily, believe me.'

'Well, it can't be anything very serious if she expects to be back on the Monday.'

I thought, not for the first time, how efficiently a village grapevine works. I supposed that absolutely everyone in Beech Green and Fairacre, if not Caxley itself, knew that Mrs Pringle was due at 'the Cottage' next Wednesday. Probably they knew why too, which was more than I did.

'It can't be appendicitis,' mused Dolly, 'she had that done some time ago. Probably just one of those tiresome women's things.'

'Mrs Partridge thinks so too,' I informed her. 'Now, do you like spring onions in your salad?'

'I shall come and help,' said Dolly, rising from her chair.

We spoke no more of Mrs Pringle.

*

'So we're going to be without Madam Sunshine, for a day or two,' said Mr Willet. 'Do you reckon we can manage?'

He gave me a sly grin.

'One thing,' he went on, 'they won't keep her any longer than they need. Hospitals these days gets you in just long enough to slit you up, stitch you up and get you up. Needs the beds, see.'

'Well, no one wants to linger anyway,' I replied.

'Linger where?' asked Mrs Pringle, appearing from the lobby.

Neither of us replied, and Bob Willet departed, rather smartly.

'One thing does worry me,' said my cleaner, 'that house of yours. I could easily give it a quick doing-over before I went in with the vicar.'

'We've had all this out already,' I told her. 'You'll have enough to do at your own place, and I can perfectly well cope for two Wednesdays.'

'I could ask Minnie,' she said. My blood ran cold. Out of pity, some time before, I had let Minnie loose in my house so that she could earn a little money, but she had nearly wrecked the place. The tea towels had been put to soak in neat bleach. She had tried to clean the windows with the stuff one uses for the insides of particularly black ovens, and I never did find the furniture polish, or the screw which holds the floor-cleaner together.

'No, don't bother Minnie,' I said hastily. 'I managed alone for years perfectly well.'

'That's as maybe,' retorted Mrs Pringle. '"Managed" perhaps. I wouldn't say "perfectly well". Never have I seen such a cupboard as that one of yours under the stairs. But there it is. Some are born tidy, and some isn't.'

I decided to be charitable and ignore these remarks.

'I shall ring the hospital on Thursday and see if you are fit to see visitors,' I replied. 'Anyway, good luck and we'll see you back on duty when you feel up to it.'

On Friday mornings, our vicar takes prayers in the school, gives a simple homily, discusses any problems with me and, all in all, is a welcome visitor.

I was able to tell him that the news from the hospital, about Mrs Pringle's affairs, was good, and that I proposed to visit her on Saturday afternoon.

He expressed relief, and then invited me to call at the vicarage after morning service on Sunday.

'Just a few old friends,' he said vaguely. 'I think you know them all, and the garden is looking at its best. Cordelia wants you to see her irises. She was so disappointed that you couldn't come the other evening.'

This, of course, caused intense feelings of guilt on my part, as I remembered my excuses about ironing and marking exercise books, when all I had attempted was the crossword, and a fine hash I had made of it, I recalled.

I promised to come and said how much I should look forward to seeing the irises, and mentally arranged a Sunday lunch which could be left to look after itself. Cold meat, or something in a casserole? Two boiled eggs would go down well, and one of the joys of living alone was the pleasure of making one's Sunday lunch as simple as that. No doubt a husband would expect a roast joint, two or three vegetables and a substantial pudding to follow. Oh, blessed spinsterhood!

On Saturday afternoon I set out for Caxley Cottage Hospital. It is situated on the outskirts of the town which is a good thing, particularly on a Saturday when Caxley High Street is choked with traffic and hundreds of shoppers intent upon committing hara-kiri by crossing the road inches in front of moving cars.

I took the back route which involves waiting at a level crossing and having a view of a small tributary of the river Kennet which runs nearby.

It is always peaceful waiting for the train to come. Small animals rustle in the reeds by the water. Wood anemones star a little copse, and in the summer meadowsweet grows in the marshy ground sending out its heady scent. In the autumn, there are some wonderful sprays of luscious blackberries at this spot, but it is hopeless to try and pick them, for no sooner are you out of the car than the gates soar up, and it is time to push on again.

This particular afternoon, the waiting was enhanced by a mallard duck who crossed the road with six yellow ducklings, halting now and again to make sure that all were in attendance. Her beady eyes looked this way and that, not I think through fear, but because she wanted to be sure that we knew that we had to wait for her. And, meekly, we did.

The hospital car park was uncomfortably full, and the usual number of thickheads had parked diagonally so that they took up two spaces instead of one. However, I edged mine beside a magnificent Mercedes and hoped for the best.

Mrs Pringle was looking resplendent in a pale blue nightgown and bright pink bed jacket. The ward seemed stiflingly hot after the fresh air, but she appeared to be quite comfortable.

'I'm doing very well considering,' she replied in answer to my enquiry into her health. 'Should be out on Monday, the sister says.'

'Will you need fetching?'

'No, my John's coming for me soon after six, and he'll run me home. Fred's been told what to get ready for me.'

131

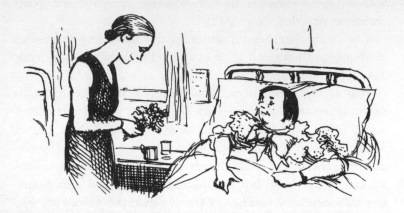

I bet he has, I thought.

'I have to see the doctor on Monday morning, just to make sure everything's holding up. Then I can have my lay-down in the afternoon, and my tea, and be ready to go home when John comes.'

I was busy gazing at the other patients during this conversation, and felt that I ought to know one woman in a nearby bed. After all, you can hardly enter 'the Cottage' without seeing someone you know. It is part of its attraction, unlike the enormous town hospitals where everyone is strange.

'Used to work in Boots,' replied Mrs Pringle in answer to my query. 'Then went on to the pork butcher's on the bridge. Nice girl. Had a brother with a hare lip.'

I returned the distant lady's smile with more confidence.

'And that woman in the next bed to her,' said Mrs Pringle, 'thinks herself the Queen of the Ward just because she's had her gall bladder out. Gets all the attention. Not that she's any worse than the rest of us, and sleeps like a log at nights, but you see she's got all her gall stones in that jam jar on the top of her cupboard, so everyone goes across to see them.'

Mrs Pringle sounded resentful of this claim to fame.

'Not that they're much to write home about,' she continued. 'Why, my Uncle Perce had one much bigger than hers, and had it on his mantelpiece. Big as a walnut it was. Always attracted notice. Made a talking point, as people say.'

'Not at meal times, I hope,' I said.

'The meals aren't bad,' said Mrs Pringle, luckily mishearing me, 'not for a hospital, I mean. We had scrambled egg for breakfast. A bit too dry, but scrambled eggs is a bit tricky if they have to be kept warm. And fish in parsley sauce for our dinner just now. At least, they said it was parsley sauce but the parsley was pretty thin on the ground. Might just as well have been cigarette ash, and maybe it was.'

I put my little offering of spring flowers on her bedspread, and there was a slight lifting of the corners of her down-turned mouth.

'Well, thank you. Not that they'll stand a chance in this heat, but it's the thought that counts, isn't it?'

'You're not in any pain, I hope?'

'Not but what I can't bear,' she said, with a martyred sigh, 'I don't take no pain-killers at night. Not like *some!*'

She cast a malevolent glance across to the gall-bladder sufferer who was now holding up her jam jar for the admiration of half a dozen visitors.

'So you'll be back on Monday,' I said hastily, to change the subject.

'Not for *work!*' she cried.

'No, no. I know you won't be fit for work for some time –' I began.

'For *some time?*' she echoed. 'Of course, I'll be back the minute I can put one foot before the other. When have you ever seen me *shirking?*'

I began to feel that I could never say the right thing, and that possibly I was making Mrs Pringle's condition worse than when I arrived.

'You *never* shirk,' I said stoutly.

'I will say one thing for this place. It may be noisy and too hot, and the pain is something cruel at times, but at least it's giving my leg a rest.'

'That's splendid,' I said. I looked at my watch. I had been by the bedside for over twenty minutes, and I felt we should both enjoy a rest from each other's company.

'I'm not going to stay any longer,' I said, 'because you need all the rest you can get. I'll pop in and see you when you have settled back at home.'

She nodded her agreement, and picked up the bunch of flowers, holding them up to her nose.

'That really do smell like Fairacre,' she cried. 'You couldn't have brought anything nicer.'

And with this rare display of grace and gratitude, she waved me away.

The next morning I gave my shoes an extra polish, my clothes an extra brush, looked out my prayer book, found finally among the cookery books, and went to morning service.

As the head mistress of a church school I ought to go every Sunday, but somehow it does not work out that way. Friends tend to invite me to share their Sunday roast, or other friends come to me from some distance, so that I do not visit St Patrick's as often as I should. Dear Gerald Partridge, however, never upbraids me, and I am grateful for his Christian forbearance.

The church, even on this sunny morning, was chilly, and I envied the sensible women who had put on knitted or tweed skirts and would be withstanding the clammy chill of the wooden pews more successfully than I was.

But the peace of the place soon exerted its customary soothing influence. The monument to Sir Charles Dagbury, who had worshipped here a few hundred years before, was as commanding as ever, but his marble curls, which cascaded to his lace collar, could have done with a dusting. Mrs Hope's little feather duster could have been useful here, I thought.

Our church is a simple structure, white-washed inside, and with a roof of stout oak beams. I remembered the magnificent fan-vaulting of Bent church at Christmas time, the beautiful carpets and the vicar's vestments.

Now Mr Partridge emerged from the vestry, followed by the ten or twelve souls forming our church choir. The four boys were all my pupils, and uncommonly angelic they looked in their snowy surplices and their hair sleeked down with a wet brush.

We began the service, and in due time settled down on our cold seats for the first lesson read by Henry Mawne.

My gaze roamed around the church. On the altar were bright garden flowers and, on each side, on the floor of the chancel, stood two large vases filled with blossom, probably from the vicarage.

I remembered the arum lilies which had flanked the chancel steps at Bent, and the plethora of exotic hothouse flowers which had scented the church that day.

St. Patrick's had no such grandeur, but it was just as moving in its homely simplicity. In both cases, honour and glory were being given.

It seemed particularly appropriate when the vicar announced the next hymn:

'Let us with a gladsome mind,
Praise the Lord for He is kind.'

It was good to get out into the sunshine again as the church clock struck twelve.

Mrs Partridge caught up with me and took my arm, waving the while with her free hand at Henry Mawne and his wife. Evidently they, and also Peter and Diana Hale from Tyler's Row, were making their way to the vicarage.

'I have my sister Edith and her husband with us for a few days,' she said, as we crunched up her drive. 'She's not been too fit, so she didn't come to church this morning. It's one of those sick headache maladies.'

I hoped she would not go into further details, and was spared as the sister in question and her husband came out of the drawing room to greet us. Both, I was relieved to see, appeared to be in robust health.

Peter Hale drifted over to me. He used to teach at Caxley Grammar School in the days when it went under that honourable name.

'This is quite a scholastic gathering, isn't it?' he said waving towards Henry Mawne with a dangerously full sherry glass, 'Cordelia's sister used to teach too, I hear.'

I enquired after his house and garden. He had bought all four cottages which comprised Tyler's Row, and was now spending his retirement improving his property.

'I must say it's absolutely engrossing, though terribly hard work. But so much more satisfying than teaching. I'd far rather lay bricks than discuss the Unification of Italy.'

'And you are now free of neighbours,' I commented. He and Diana had suffered much when they first bought the property, for Mrs Fowler, a virago of a widow, had lived next door in the end cottage, and had made their lives a misery.

'Thank heaven for that!' he said. 'I hear she is living in Caxley, and I don't envy her neighbours there, I must say.'

At this point the Mawnes came up and enquired after Mrs Pringle. I told them about my visit, sticking to the fact of the lady's good recovery, and her hopes to be home the next day.

'Not a bad hospital that,' commented Henry. 'They did a good job on my hydraulic system.'

'Well, we don't want to hear about *that*, Henry,' said his wife severely. He seemed unabashed.

'Then I'll tell you about a spotted woodpecker that comes regularly to our bird table,' he said with a smile. And he did.

Soon Mrs Partridge led us into the garden. She is one of those gardeners, maddening to the rest of us, who never seem to have any set-backs – if Cordelia Partridge plants anything, it grows. Even those most tricky of bulbs, the nerines, which bloom in October and November, flourish in the vicarage garden and supply the house with beautiful pink blooms when the rest of Fairacre is doing its best with hardy chrysanthemums.

The irises, of course, were superb. I was not expecting anything quite so foreign-looking as the dark brown and yellow, the burgundy and cream, and even a two-coloured beauty in pale mauve which delighted our eyes. Cordelia Partridge was suitably smug with the praise heaped upon her, and we were allowed to wander at will after we had paid our respects to the iris bed.

I found myself by the rockery in the company of Diana Hale.

'It must be a mixed blessing for you having Mrs Pringle back again.'

'That's true,' I admitted.

'One thing about her,' went on Diana Hale, 'she is the only person I ever met who could compete with our awful Mrs Fowler. They crossed swords once outside the Post Office, and I've never seen such a clash! I slunk home the other way, too scared to go near them. But I must say, it did my heart good to see Mrs Fowler being trounced.'

'Oh, she's a doughty fighter, is Mrs Pringle,' I said. 'I know that to my cost.'

But somehow, I thought as I made my way home to a late lunch, I should be quite glad to see the old harridan when she deigned to turn up.

It dawned on me later that I still had no idea of the cause of Mrs Pringle's visit to 'the Cottage'.

What is more, I had no intention of enquiring.

CHAPTER 11

Rumours and Conflicts

As it happened, Mrs Pringle did not appear again until the week after her return.

Apart from the limp she seemed as tough as ever, and quite disappointed to find that both the school and my house had survived without her attentions.

However, she cheered up when she studied the children's wash basins which she pronounced 'a death trap swarming with germs', and attacked them with Vim and plenty of elbow grease. She was positively genial when this task was over, and told me that the hospital had given her a diet sheet.

'The doctor there said I was to lose two stone. But if I stuck to his diet I'd be in my grave by Christmas. All greenery and acid fruit, and what they calls "roughage" and I calls "animal feed". All them oats and raw carrots and apples! Never heard the like. I told him flat: "My sister was warned against just such a diet when she had colitis. Funny we never hear about colitis these days – just this 'ere roughage."'

'And what did he say?'

'Oh, you know doctors! He just waved it aside, and said

to keep off sugar, fat and starches. And I said: "And what does that leave, pray, for a hard-working woman?" He simply walked away. I mean, it's so *rude*. Some of these so-called educated men what's been to college and that, haven't got any more manners than Minnie Pringle's boy Basil. And that's saying something.'

I was foolish enough to enquire after Minnie, and Mrs Pringle's face grew sourer than ever.

'Her husband Ern's playing up,' she said, 'getting home late, and sometimes staying out all night. He's been seen in Caxley too.'

She made Caxley sound like Sodom and Gomorrah rolled into one.

'Mind you,' she continued, 'our Minnie's no home-maker, and you can't blame the chap in some ways. You should see Minnie's cooking! Burnt pies, addled custard, potatoes full of eyes, and the house filthy with it.'

'Still, that's no excuse for neglecting a wife, surely?'

'It's plain you don't know *nothing* about *men*!' she retorted, and limped away.

Later that morning some rhythmic thuds which disturbed the comparative peace of our Arithmetic lesson took me into the playground to investigate.

I found Mr Willet, mallet in hand, thumping at the gate-post.

'Bit out of true,' he told me, desisting for a moment. 'Why, can you hear me in there?'

'That's why I've come out,' I said. 'I wondered if Mr Roberts had got one of those confounded bangers going in the field.'

'What, a bird-scarer?'

'That's right.'

140

'Don't do a ha'porth of good, them things. Besides it's the wrong time of year for that lark.'

'I'd better get back,' I said, 'before there's a riot.'

'Heard about the Russells?'

These were fairly recent arrivals in Fairacre, and I had three of their children at school.

'No. What?'

'Been made redundant, if that's the right word. Stood off anyway. Last come, first go, evidently.'

'I didn't quite take in what he did do.'

'Something to do with machines in Caxley. Make the bits they do there, in some back alley running down to the river.'

'That's tough on him,' I said, 'and I shall miss the children. They're a nice little lot.'

Bob Willet looked at me with an unusually solemn expression.

'You knows what this means? The numbers get fewer every term. Looks to me as though the office will be closing us down. We'll both be out of a job, you'll see. Like poor Stan Russell.'

'I doubt it,' I told him. 'And anyway, this school has been threatened with closure ever since I've been here. We've always fought it off. We'll do it again if need be.'

I could hear the sound of voices coming from my classroom. No doubt warfare was about to break out.

'Must go,' I said, and hastened away to quell the riot.

Despite my brave words to Bob Willet, I felt a certain tremor about this latest piece of news, and wondered what the future would hold.

During the next few hours I heard the same tale from the vicar, Mr Lamb and Mrs Pringle. All three added their

141

own gloomy prognostications about the possibility of Fair-acre School closing if numbers fell further.

The evening was overcast, and now that the autumn was upon us the days were shorter. I could not rid myself of a feeling of foreboding as I sat, red pencil in hand, correcting essays and changing 'brids' to 'birds' and 'grils' to 'girls' with depressing regularity. 'Off of', 'meet up with' and 'never had none', also cropped up here and there, and after a while I put aside my work and made myself a cup of coffee. It was supposed to be a stimulant, and I could do with it.

I faced the various possibilities which my future might hold if Mr Willet's forecast proved correct. The obvious one would be a transfer to another school, or I could apply for a post elsewhere. On the other hand, I could take early retirement, but should I really like that?

I lived in a tied house which went with the job. Presumably the education authority would put it up for sale, as it would the school building itself.

Normally this would have been the most serious blow, for I had certainly not enough money to buy another, and had been foolish enough not to acquire one over the years, as some prudent teachers did when contemplating retirement.

But this worry was spared me, for a year or two earlier Dolly Clare had told me that she had left her Beech Green cottage to me in her will. This overwhelmingly generous deed had lifted the fears of the future from my undeserving shoulders. I should not be homeless whenever the blow fell, for Dolly had stipulated that I could stay with her whenever I liked, and however short the notice. To be so spoilt touched me deeply, and I knew that I should never be able to repay my old friend as she deserved.

Naturally, we had agreed that nothing would be said by either of us. Miss Clare's solicitor had the legal side of the transaction drawn up, but Dolly and I preserved strict silence about the matter.

Nevertheless, as the months passed, I grew conscious of the fact that the disposition of Dolly's main asset was known in the neighbourhood. How, or why, or by whom this knowledge was transmitted, neither of us could imagine. But we had both heard a remark here and there, noticed a knowing look, a nod of the head and so on, which made it clear that this piece of news was airborne like the seeds of thistledown, and lodged just as tenaciously wherever it happened to alight. Was *everything* known in a village, I wondered, sipping my coffee?

Echo answered: 'Of course it is!'

I was about to take my worries to bed when the telephone rang. It was Amy, offering me early plums.

'Rather sharp, from a funny old tree, but they make lovely jelly. Like some?'

I said that I should.

'You sound mopey,' said Amy. 'Are you ill or something?'

'No, no. Just tired. I've been marking essays.'

'Well, you should be used to that. I'll pop over tomorrow after school and bring the plums. What's more, I'll bring some crumpets for tea. It's getting quite nippy when the sun goes down, and crumpets are wonderfully cheering.'

'You are a stout friend,' I told her sincerely, 'and I'll look forward to seeing you and the crumpets tomorrow.'

'I'd better warn you, I have a new car. It's automatic, and I only hope I can manage it from Bent to Fairacre. I'll come the back way, so if I'm not with you by four-thirty you'll know where to direct the search party.'

And on this practical note I went to bed, much cheered.

By the morning, of course, I was feeling much more hopeful. As I had said to Bob Willet, we were quite accustomed to the threat of closure, and there was no reason to suppose that the departure of the three Russell children would make much difference. With any luck, I told myself in my present buoyant mood, we should have another family with children moving into Fairacre.

I might have guessed that Fate was waiting to have another crack at me. My assistant, who had been in the infants' classroom as Miss Briggs for some time, was now Mrs Richards, and still doing sterling work.

She now approached me with unusual diffidence and told me that the doctor had confirmed her hopes and that she was pregnant.

'Oh dear!' I said involuntarily, and then hastily added congratulations, and asked when the baby was due.

'Early March,' she said. 'If all goes well, I thought I could work until half-term in February, and then give up.'

'But you'll come back later?' I queried. She was a good teacher and we had always got on well together. In a two-teacher school this relationship is extra important, and I must admit I have had so many changes over the years that I dreaded yet another.

'I'm not sure,' she said, 'it all depends on how I feel when the time comes. I shall certainly take the full maternity leave, but of course I'll be in touch to let you know how things are going.'

'Fair enough,' I replied. 'But I hope you will return. I've enjoyed your company.'

'That goes for me too,' she said, 'and Wayne says will you be godmother?'

'My goodness,' I cried, quite overcome by this, 'I think it's a bit early to decide on that, but yes, if you still feel the same way next March I should count it an honour.'

'We shan't change our minds.'

'Well, I think you should choose the hymn this morning in celebration.'

'What about "Praise to the Holiest in the height"?' she replied with a smile.

'Very suitable,' I agreed, putting my fears behind me. Trust *Hymns Ancient and Modern* to come up with something fitting!

It was good to see Amy, as always. She arrived at ten past four, complete with plums and crumpets, so that I did not have to organise a search party as we had feared.

The car was discreetly opulent as befitted a tycoon's wife and I was greatly intrigued with the automatic controls.

'Jolly useful if you break your left leg,' I said, 'or your left arm for that matter.'

'It might well be your right, of course,' commented Amy, 'or both. Then what would you do?'

'I should sell it, and put the money aside for taxis,' I told her. 'Let's go and toast these crumpets.'

'Now tell me what was worrying you yesterday,' said Amy later, licking a buttery finger.

I told her about the Russell children and Mr Willet's gloomy forecast.

'Well, that's something that's been hanging over you for years,' she said. 'The snag is, you'd have to give up this house, I suppose.'

'I don't think I should actually be thrown out. I'd have plenty of time to look around. The office is pretty humane, and I've been here for long enough for them to know me.'

I always feel guilty about keeping my secret from Amy, but I stick to the sensible principle of letting no one – no matter how trustworthy – learn of something which one does not want disclosed. In all innocence it can be let out, and it is a burden which one should not lay on anyone's shoulders. The old adage: 'Least said, soonest mended' is one I live by, and as a villager it is doubly true. Of course, this is a puny adversary compared with the local grapevine but it is a useful principle to adopt.

'You should have bought something years ago,' said Amy, with a return of her usual bossy tone.

'I know,' I said meekly.

'Well, if you do get the push,' she continued, helping herself to another crumpet, 'there's always our spare bedroom. The curtains clash rather with the carpet, but I don't suppose you'd notice.'

As we washed up, she admired a large bowl of red and green tomatoes which Alice Willet had brought for me.

'For chutney?' she asked.

'Only the green ones. I shall freeze a few of the red ones, and have a feast for the next few days with the others. Would you like some?'

'Please. It's funny, I could never bear tomatoes as a child, or beetroot, or swedes. Now I dote on all three.'

'I can't face the last,' I said, 'nothing more than shredded soap. We get far too many swedes at school dinners during the winter, but thank heaven the children like them.'

'When you are out of work,' said Amy, hanging up the tea towel, 'and begging in the wintry streets of Caxley, you'll be glad of a nice plate of hot swedes handed out at the soup kitchen.'

'I'll just ask for the soup.'

'You'll have what you are given,' Amy told me severely, 'as our mothers used to say.'

'As long as our benefactors don't add that old bit about "thousands of poor children",' I answered, 'I'll accept anything gratefully, but I draw the line at swedes.'

It was about this time that Mrs Pringle's limp became so apparent that I was impelled to ask after her leg.

'Too much to do. that's my trouble,' she told me. 'Top and bottom of it is Minnie.'

'Hasn't Ern come back?'

'No. He's still in Caxley, and the worst of it is that Bert's hanging around her again – always was dead set on Minnie.'

'She must send him packing.'

'Fat chance of that. I can see the girl's lonely without Ern, but she's far too soft to give Bert the push. And what's more, she's everlasting coming up to my place, mooning about with all those kids. I've had more than enough, I can tell you. The minute I finds out where Ern is in Caxley I'm going to fetch him back.'

'Can't the police trace him?'

'No one wants to get mixed up with *the police*,' she said, with such disgust that one felt that she looked upon that noble force as being on a par with some virulent germ.

'Well, I should make sure Minnie doesn't worry you,' I said, 'after all, you haven't got your strength back yet from the operation.'

This seemed to mollify the lady, and she nodded her head in agreement.

'Well, we must see what comes to pass,' she said, attacking my Victorian ink stand with a dab of Brasso.

What came to pass was the appearance of Mrs Pringle, a few days later, with a scratch on one cheek, bruises on her face, and a bump on her head.

'Have you had a fall?' I asked, much alarmed. 'I think you should see a doctor.'

'No need for that. These wounds was come by in Righteous Battle,' she replied. 'And my enemy come off worse, I can tell you.'

'But who?'

She settled herself on the front desk and folded her arms across the flowered overall which is her working garb.

'It was like this. Minnie suddenly let out that Ern was staying in Caxley with – you'll never guess!'

She looked at me bright-eyed.

'His mother?' I hazarded.

She snorted with disgust.

'Ern's mother has been dead these ten years. No, I tell a

lie. Must be nearer twelve, because she came to the chapel centenary, and very poorly she looked then, we all thought.'

'Then I've no idea,' I said firmly. I set about looking for a pen knife I needed in the desk drawer. This withdrawal of my interest spurred Mrs Pringle into action again.

'That Mrs Fowler! You know, as used to be at Tyler's Row before it was prettied up. I never could stand that woman, and she was proper insulting to me on more than one occasion.'

'Did Minnie get in touch with her somehow?'

'No. I said I'd get in touch!' Mrs Pringle's tone was triumphant. 'That Minnie wouldn't say boo to a goose. But the minute she told me Ern was there as a lodger – *so-called* – I thought I'll get that fellow back before the night's out. I've had enough of Minnie and her tribe under my feet all day. If Ern's back, he'll have to look after them, and he can see off that good-for-nothing Bert who's hanging round Minnie all the time, and confusing her.'

In my opinion, Minnie's state of confusion is permanent, but I forbore to comment.

'So,' said Mrs Pringle, sitting down heavily on the creaking desk, 'I caught the Caxley and went straight to her place. When she opened the door I said I wanted Ern and wasn't going until she handed him over.'

'Was he there then? I should have thought he would be at work.'

Mrs Pringle tut-tutted at this interruption, and I fell silent.

'She said she hadn't got him, had never wanted him, he never paid the rent, and he was at "The Barleycorn" round the corner. And then she said something *so rude* about me I wouldn't soil my lips by repeating. So I slapped her face.'

149

'That was very . . .' I paused, not knowing whether to say 'brave' or 'foolhardy', and Mrs Pringle rushed on.

'So she grabbed at me and that's where I got this nasty scratch on my face, the vixen. It was then I clawed out a good handful of her hair. She shrieked something terrible, but I told her she'd asked for it.'

Joseph Coggs put his head round the classroom door at this point, asking if he could ring the bell. We waved him away.

'I was just going down the path to the gate when that besom opened the top window and flung Ern's case out. It hit me on the top of my head. Might have killed me as I told her at the time. That's what brought up this wicked great lump on my head.'

'Did you find Ern?'

'I did indeed. He was at "The Barleycorn" all right, with a lot of his layabout cronies. I shoved the case at him and brought him home. Just caught the last Fairacre luckily.'

My mind boggled at such meekness on Ern's part, and I said so.

'I never had a mite of trouble with him,' Mrs Pringle said, standing up and stroking down her flowered overall. 'Ern's a great coward for all his bluster. To tell the truth, I reckon I went there at just the right time. He and Mrs Fowler was at loggerheads already, and he was scared to go back there, I reckon. That woman can be quite violent at times.'

I looked at Mrs Pringle's battle scars and agreed.

'So you think he'll settle down again with Minnie?'

'Who's to say?' She began to set off for the lobby. 'But I done my bit last night. It's up to them to make it up.'

A rare smile crossed her battered countenance.

'One thing, that Mrs Fowler won't be feeling too grand today. I smote her good and proper, like they did the wicked in the Bible.'

'Tell Joe he can come in and ring the bell,' I called after her.

And about time too, I thought, looking at the clock.

I had just returned to the school house that afternoon, and had decided to light the fire as a nasty little cold wind had blown up when I heard tapping at the back door.

There stood Minnie Pringle. For once, she was un-encumbered with a pram and toddlers. She looked re-markably waif-like shivering in the wind.

'Come in,' I cried. 'Do you want Mrs Pringle? She doesn't come here on a Friday, you know.'

151

'Auntie don't know about me coming,' she replied.

'Sit down, while I put a match to this fire,' I said.

She obeyed, sitting primly on the edge of a Victorian buttoned chair which is liable to tip forward unless its occupier sits well back.

I pointed this out to Minnie but it seemed to have no meaning to her, and she remained dangerously perched.

'Well, what brings you here today, Minnie? And where are the children?'

'My mum at Springbourne has 'em Friday afternoons. She does the ironing from the Manor then. She irons lovely.'

'Lovelily,' I corrected automatically, ever the teacher. It did not sound right.

'Beautifully,' I amended hastily.

'That's right. Lovely,' agreed Minnie. I let it pass.

'Ern's back,' she said, after a pause.

'Good,' I said, wondering whether to commiserate or congratulate.

'Bert don't like it,' she added.

This, I felt, was hardly surprising, but made a noncommittal noise. I was tired, cold and dying for a cup of tea.

'I'm about to make tea,' I said, facing the fact that Minnie would be with me for some time yet, 'would you like a cup?'

'Lovely,' said Minnie. 'Shall I help?'

'No, no. You sit there and get warm.'

I looked at the lightweight suit she was wearing. It was a dazzling turquoise blue with grubby white trimmings. Her stick-like arms, mottled with the cold, protruded from the sleeves. It could have done with Minnie's mother's ironing expertise.

'You should have put on a coat,' I said, as I waited for the kettle to come to my rescue.

'It's on the baby's pram,' she replied. Whether it was there to keep the baby warm, or because Minnie had put it there and forgotten to retrieve it, I was never to know, for the kettle whistled and I attended to my duties as hostess.

Over our steaming cups and a ginger biscuit apiece, Minnie became more relaxed.

'I wondered if I could come and work for you Fridays,' she said.

My heart sank.

'Isn't there somewhere nearer to find work?' I said, playing for time. 'Surely you used to have a job at Springbourne Manor?'

'They don't want nobody at that house,' she said.

And I don't want nobody at this house, I thought. It all seemed pretty hard. Dash it all, I already suffered Mrs Pringle on a Wednesday. To have Friday afternoon commandeered as well was really rather much. In any case, what on earth could I let Minnie do which she could manage without causing irreparable damage? I had faced this problem before, with small success.

'You see,' said Minnie, placing her tea-cup in the hearth by the side, rather than on the saucer, 'I run up a bill at Springbourne Stores when Ern was away, and I needs the money.'

'Can't Ern pay it?'

'He says I done it and I got to pay it back.'

I looked at the pinched face, the tousled red hair, the cheap flimsy shoes. She might have been taken for an

153

under-nourished child of twelve, rather than a wife and mother of three.

I began to feel my tough old heart softening a little. After all, she had had the initiative to walk from Spring-bourne and to apply for a job.

'It's like this, Minnie,' I told her, 'I can really only afford to have you for an hour on a Friday. Your Aunt Maud does all that's really needed on Wednesday, as I'm sure you know.'

'That'd suit me fine,' said Minnie, looking more cheer-ful.

'And I'm not making it a permanent arrangement,' I went on, gaining strength. 'If you like to come, say, until we break up for Christmas, then you are welcome, but I don't want too much help over the holidays.'

'What time?' said Minnie, beginning to stand up ready for departure. 'My cousin comes up to help in the garden at Mr Mawne's Friday afternoons. He'd give me a lift in his van. Has to be there at two o'clock.'

'That will suit me,' I said, 'then you can go at three.'

That way, I figured, I should not have to share the house with her. At the same time, I reminded myself, I should probably have to spend half an hour or so clearing up after Minnie's labours.

A gust of wind flung a spattering of dry leaves against the window as I showed her to the door.

'Lor!' said Minnie, flinching from the cold wind as we opened the back door.

'Hang on,' I said, 'you'd better have a cardigan.'

I scrabbled under the stairs in the cupboard which Mrs Pringle so greatly deplores, and emerged with a thick cardigan which was there with other garments waiting for the next local jumble sale.

'Thanks ever so,' cried Minnie, when safely enveloped, 'I'll bring it back Friday. See you then.'

She gave me her mad grin and teetered down the path in the dilapidated shoes.

'Tibby,' I said to the cat who was stretched in comfort before the fire, 'I am not only an ass, but what Mr Willet rightly calls "a soft touch".'

And what, I suddenly thought with alarm, should I say to Mrs Pringle?

CHAPTER 12

The End of the Year

I need not have worried. Mrs Pringle knew all about Minnie's new job when our paths crossed on Monday morning, and she was far from pleased.

'I suppose you knows what you are doing,' was her opening gambit, 'but what, pray, are you going to find for Minnie to do on a Friday?'

This problem had been facing me over the weekend, and I trotted out a few ideas.

'She can wash the porch floors,' I said, 'those quarry tiles are pretty tough. And she could do the kitchen floor while she's about it. It would save you doing it.'

Mrs Pringle snorted. 'Minnie's not to be let loose on my kitchen floor, and anyway she'd ruin that squeegie-thing you got me. If Minnie does the kitchen floor, I goes, I tell you flat.'

'Very well, if that's how you feel,' I said, with what dignity I could muster, 'but she's certainly going to do the porches. And I'm sure she could manage the brass and copper. And even the silver,' I added, getting bolder.

'In that case, you'd have to put it out separate,' she said. 'Brasso, copper and brass one week. Silvo and the silver next, or you'll be in a fine old mess. Worse than usual, I mean,' she added vindictively.

'Well, it's only for a few weeks,' I said, 'just up until Christmas. She seemed to need the money, and I thought it was very resourceful of her to come and try her luck.'

'You'll rue it!' she said darkly, waddling off to the infants' room.

For the next few Fridays I tried to nip across from the school to the house to see that Minnie was safely started on her set jobs. Washing the floors of the front and back porch she managed very well, but I had to be sure that she only used harmless but efficient soap liquid. This was the only bottle I left out for her, and I forbade her to take anything from the cleaning cupboard.

I knew that she could not read, so hid such dangerous things as disinfectant, bleach and scouring agents in case she used – or even drank – them during her labours.

By dint of putting out the Brasso, copper and brass together on the kitchen table one week, and Silvo and my meagre collection of silver and plated articles the next, as advised by Mrs Pringle, things went fairly smoothly, but there were some aspects of Minnie's ministrations which I was unable to alter.

Long before I had met her, she had been taught to wash her dusters and to leave them to dry before returning home. This excellent training had stuck in Minnie's feather brain, and the dusters were always spotless when I returned from school.

Unfortunately, I was unable to get it into Minnie's thick skull that they should be hung on a little line outside the back door to dry. In Minnie's past, dusters were always put to dry indoors, and I found my own draped over the edge of the dining room table, the banisters, and even over the backs of upholstered chairs.

I always intended to point this out to Minnie, but often, by the next Friday, I had forgotten. It was useless to leave notes for her as she could not read, but I had not really taken in the fact that she could not tell the time, until I found her still in the house well after the hour when she should have departed.

'Well, I never sort of mastered the clock,' she said vaguely, implying that there were a great many other things which she *had* mastered in her time.

'But how do you manage?' I enquired, genuinely interested.

'I looks out for the Caxley,' she replied. 'It gets to the church about the hour.'

'But not *every* hour,' I pointed out.

'There's the kids coming out of school, too,' she explained.

'It still seems rather hit and miss,' I said, 'and there are lots of places where you can't see the bus, or the children for that matter. Has Springbourne Church got a striking clock? Can you hear it at home?'

'I never bothers to count,' replied Minnie. 'Sometimes I misses the first note or so.'

It began to seem more and more difficult to me.

'Actually,' said Minnie, 'I just asks somebody the time.'

I did not have to wait long before the comments on Minnie Pringle's return arrived.

Mr Willet was the first.

'You could've knocked me down with a feather when Alice told me Minnie was back. "Never!" I said to her. "Miss Read had enough last time. She's got too much

savvy to have Minnie back again." But there you are! I see
you've been taken advantage of.'

This last sentence annoyed me on two counts. Firstly, it
was ungrammatical, ending with a preposition as it did.
Secondly, it seemed to put me on a par with all those
gullible girls who are the victims of predatory males.

'It's only until Christmas,' I told him rather coldly.

'She can do plenty of damage before then,' he commented, and continued with his coke-sweeping.

The vicar said that it was a great credit to me to employ
Minnie and that he was sure the girl must be most grateful.

Mrs Partridge, more of a realist, begged me to keep any
breakables out of Minnie's clutches.

'She *once* – and I stress *once*,' she told me, 'helped wash
up after a Fur and Feather Whist Drive in the village hall,
and we lost four plates, three cups and a sandwich dish
which unfortunately belonged to Mrs Pringle. I had a great
deal of trouble trying to replace it, and she did not seem to
appreciate it when we did track one down.'

I said that I could well believe it.

Mr Lamb said Minnie was a very lucky girl. Mrs Willet
said Bob could have been knocked down with a feather.
Mrs Richards, now in a capacious maternity smock, confessed herself amazed, Amy, on the telephone, responded
to my news with: 'What on earth are you thinking about?',
and even gentle Miss Clare, when I visited her, advised me
not to let my heart rule my head.

It was all pretty hard to bear, but I only had myself to
blame, and comforted myself with the thought that Christmas would soon be here, and my bonds would be broken.

It began to grow very cold. Rough winds which had
chased the dead leaves round and round the playground,

and sent their most searching draughts down the skylight, now gave way to still weather of biting chill.

I shivered in my bedroom as I dressed each morning by the inadequate heat of an electric fire, and thought of Amy and many other lucky women, who had central heating in their homes.

I routed out my warmest clothes, regretting the thick cardigan which I had given to Minnie as the only one which had really matched my thickest skirt. This sort of thing is always happening.

And ten to one, I told myself, as I had never seen Minnie wearing my garment, it was on the baby's pram with her own coat. Unless, of course, she too had passed it on to a jumble sale.

It was good to get home after school and to settle in by a roaring fire, knowing that the frost was sparkling outside behind the drawn curtains.

I even changed my late night cup of coffee for one of milky cocoa, remembering Dolly Clare's account of this warming drink so much appreciated by long-ago Fairacre children.

Tibby enjoyed this too, and lapped at a saucerful in the hearth while I sipped mine with my feet up on the sofa.

'You wants to take your spade inside tonight,' Bob Willet called out to me one afternoon. 'You see! There'll be snow afore mornin'.'

I have a great respect for Mr Willet's weather lore, and although I did not take the garden spade indoors, I certainly found the coal shovel and put it ready with my wellington boots.

He was right, of course. It was a white world in the morning. The trees were bowed with their burden, the garden beds hidden beneath their white blanket, and the distant downs shrouded as far as the eye could see.

Snow was still falling. It lay thick upon the window sills, and crusted the ledges of each windowpane. I dressed hurriedly, congratulating myself on looking out that shovel which I should need to get out of the back door.

Nothing moved in the garden. No birds hovered round the bird table. No doubt they were sheltering from the snow flakes in the hedgerows and buildings.

From the kitchen window, as I prepared porridge for breakfast as the best possible warmer on such a day, I could see Tibby's footmarks, a ribbon of rosettes in the snow, leading to the cat flap. The cat's fur was still flecked with melting flakes when we greeted each other.

I cleared the back and front steps just enough to let me open the doors, but I could see it was going to be love's labour lost with the snow still falling. With wellingtons on, my thickest coat buttoned up, and an umbrella atop, I fought my way over the virgin wastes to the school.

Footsteps led from the road into the building, and Mrs Pringle was already there stoking the stoves.

'No children yet,' I observed.

'Nor likely to be,' she replied, 'there's a fair old drift at the end of the lane. Mr Roberts give me a lift up in his Land Rover.'

Here was a dilemma. How was I to get her back after her labours? I knew that I should never be able to dig the snow away from my garage doors, let alone negotiate the drift in the lane with my small car.

As if she could read my thoughts, she continued: 'Mr Roberts and his shepherd's going by with the Land Rover in half an hour, when Mr Roberts has had his breakfast. Says I can squeeze in the cab with them two.'

A squeeze, I thought, it certainly would be.

'Why not go over to the school house,' I said, 'when

161

you have done here. The fire's going, and as soon as this snow lets up, I'll get you home somehow.'

'No, no. I'll go with Mr Roberts. I've got to get back. I've got Fred in bed with his chest.'

He would hardly be in bed without it, I commented mentally, but kept this flippancy to myself.

She bustled about humming some dirge while I found the register and wondered if I should have any attendances to mark in it.

At that moment the telephone rang and I snatched it from the cupboard top to hear Mrs Richards' voice.

'Absolutely impossible to make it,' she said, 'even in Wayne's van. The road between Beech Green and Fairacre's waist deep.'

I told her not to worry, and said that I did not think we should have many pupils, and that I should be ringing the office after nine to say that I intended to close the school.

'And what about my stoves?' demanded Mrs Pringle, who should not have been eavesdropping on the conversation. 'Another full week we've got before end of term. Who's to keep 'em going? Or do we let 'em out?'

'Look,' I said, 'be reasonable. How do I know? All I propose to do is to play it by ear. I shall stay here until mid-morning in case some children do get through, and they can have a bite to eat in my house, as obviously the dinner van will never make it. I shall ring the office any minute now, as *you heard*,' I added pointedly, 'and I'll tell you before you go home.'

At that moment there was a flurry at the door and Ernest, who lives nearest to the school, appeared caked in snow all down his coat, but with a pink shining face and bright eyes.

'Get out!' shouted Mrs Pringle.

'Shake your coat outside,' I said more mildly, 'and leave your wellingtons in the lobby. Then come and get warm.'

Sniffing cheerfully, he obeyed.

'I shoved along under the hedge,' he said, when he was holding his hands over the stove. 'It ain't too bad there, in the shelter, see?'

'Anyone else in sight?'

'Not a sausage,' said my lone pupil.

The telephone rang again. It was a message from the office to say that closure of the schools in our downland area was inevitable. We chatted about the weather conditions: a bus had overturned in Caxley High Street making everyday confusion even more confounded, no one could get over the downs to Oxford in the north or Winchester in the south, the farmers were fearing for their sheep, and the best thing to do was to sit by the fire.

I relayed this invigorating news to Mrs Pringle who began to swathe herself in layers of clothing ready for her homeward ride. There was a sound of voices shouting and a well-revved engine chugging, and Mrs Pringle set off for the door.

'Expect me when you see me,' she boomed, 'and look after yourself.'

It was very quiet when she had gone. Ernest looked apprehensive. 'D'you reckon any of the others will get here?'

'I doubt it, Ernest. Is your mother at home?'

'Not till ten. She goes down the Post Office to help with old Mrs Lamb, nine till ten. Blanket bath and that.'

I remembered that Ernest's mother had once been a district nurse.

'Well, you go and find something to read from the cupboard,' I said, 'and I'll see you home just after ten.'

I had a brainwave and rang the Post Office.

'Yes,' said Mr Lamb, 'Ern's mum made it across the back field. Jolly stout effort. We'll get her home, never fear, by ten.'

'Any sign of children coming to school?'

'Not one,' he told me.

'Spread the news that school's closed till further notice,' I said.

We exchanged pleasurably dramatic news. Up to the eaves down Pig Lane where the wind caught it. Two abandoned cars outside 'The Beetle and Wedge'. Bob Willet had sent a message to say he'd be up school as soon as he could make it. Some old tramp had been found sleeping in the church porch, and the vicar had taken him home; Mrs Vicar wasn't best pleased; fleas and that. No sign of Mr Roberts' sheep in Long Meadow, probably under the snow.

He rang off at last, leaving me with hazy memories of *Lorna Doone* and gurt Jan Ridd rescuing his flock.

'Makes a bit of fun, don't it?' said Ernest happily.

We were snowbound for the rest of that week, and the thaw came slowly, leaving piles of snow at the sides of the lanes and under the field hedges. The roads were filthy, churned up during daylight by farm transport and the occasional lorry or Land Rover. At night everything froze solid again. It was a bitter spell.

School re-opened on the last Monday morning of term, but a number of children still stayed away, some because travelling was impossible, others the victims of coughs and colds. Our usual Christmas party, for parents and friends, was postponed to sometime in the New Year.

Bob Willet, muffled to the eyebrows, was busy clearing the playground as I walked across. A few children were making their way to the school door, one kicking a snow-ball before him.

'Now then!' shouted Mr Willet sternly. 'Lay off that lark!'

I smiled my approval, wondering the while about the idiocy of some of our daily utterances. Why 'Now then'? And 'there, there' was pretty silly too, when analysed.

I pushed open the door into the lobby. Mrs Pringle, bucket at her feet and floor cloth in her hand, stood there, looking grim.

Before I could make any greeting, she jerked her head towards the footprints I had made on the floor.

'I just done that,' she said flatly, and all at once I was

transported back to my first encounter with Mrs Pringle
one wet July afternoon all those years ago – when she
greeted me in the self-same place and with the self-same
words: 'I just done that.'

That last skirmish with Mrs Pringle happened an hour
ago, and I shall not dwell on it. She has not changed over
the years, and is not likely to now.

Outside the snow still falls. The playground, which Bob
Willet cleared so recently, is white again, and the sky looks
menacing. But here, in the school house, all is snug and
quiet. The fire crackles, Tibby purrs, and soon I shall make
some tea. The Christmas holidays lie ahead, and what a
comforting thought that is!

Meanwhile, I must stir myself to wrap up a box of
chocolates, my annual present to Mrs Pringle.

After all, this is the season of peace and goodwill.

ABOUT THE AUTHOR

Miss Read is actually Mrs. Dora Saint, whose novels draw on her own memories of living and teaching in a small English village. She first began writing after the Second World War, mainly light essays about school and country matters, for several journals. Her first book, *Village School,* was published in England by Michael Joseph and then in the United States by Houghton Mifflin Company in 1955. She has since delighted millions of readers with both the Fairacre series and her equally well loved series about the Cotswold village of Thrush Green. Miss Read and her husband, a retired schoolmaster, have one daughter and enjoy a quiet life near Newbury, Berkshire.

Available in paperback
from the beloved Fairacre series

Village School "An affectionate, humorous, and gently charming chronicle."
— *New York Times*

The first novel in the Fairacre series, *Village School* introduces us to that cheerful schoolmistress Miss Read and her lovable group of children, who are just as likely to lose themselves as their mittens. ISBN 0-618-12702-X, $12.00

Village Centenary "Miss Read reminds us of what is really important."
— *USA Today*

Village Centenary chronicles the year Miss Read's school celebrates its one hundredth anniversary with the help — and, in some cases, hindrance — of many of our favorite Fairacre friends. ISBN 0-618-12703-8, $12.00

Summer at Fairacre "A world of innocent integrity in almost perfect prose consisting of wit, humor and wisdom in equal measure." — *Cleveland Plain Dealer*

Summer at Fairacre charmingly recounts one hot — but very welcome — summer, when Miss Read tends to the problems and possibilities that unfold in the lives of her downland village friends against the background of Albertine roses, skylarks, and bees. ISBN 0-618-12704-6, $12.00

Changes at Fairacre "Fairacre offers a restful change from the frenetic pace of the contemporary world." *Publishers Weekly*

While Fairacre's new commuter lifestyle causes a sharp decline in enrollment at Miss Read's school, Miss Read focuses her attention on the ill health of her old friend Dolly Clare. ISBN 0-618-15457-4, $12.00

Farewell to Fairacre "Humor guides her pen but charity steadies it . . . Delightful." — *Times Literary Supplement*

The beloved village schoolmistress, Miss Read, is suddenly taken ill and must consider leaving her longtime post at the school. But through the changing seasons in this gentle, humorous drama, the problems of Miss Read and her fellow residents of Fairacre are gradually resolved.

ISBN 0-618-15456-6, $12.00